camp
alien

Camp ALiEN

pameLa F. Service

illustrated by **mike gorman**

BOOK #2 OF THE
aLien agent
series.

Carolrhoda Books · Minneapolis · New York

Carolrhoda Books
A division of Lerner Publishing Group, Inc.
241 First Avenue North
Minneapolis, MN 55401 U.S.A.

Website address: www.lernerbooks.com

Library of Congress Cataloging-in-Publication Data

Service, Pamela F.
    Camp alien / by Pamela F. Service ; illustrated by Mike Gorman.
       p.   cm. — (Alien agent)
    Summary: Young alien agent Zack, surly Galactic Patrol Cadet Vraj, and shy human
camper Opal team up to find some Duthwi eggs before they hatch and cause a planetwide
disaster, while the Gnairt who were smuggling the eggs try to retrieve them.
    ISBN 978-0-8225-8656-2 (trade hard cover : alk. paper)
    [1. Extraterrestrial beings—Fiction. 2. Camps—Fiction. 3. Smuggling—Fiction.
4. Science fiction. 5. Humorous stories.] I. Gorman, Mike, ill. II. Title.
PZ7.S4885Cam 2009
[Fic]—dc22   2008020555

Manufactured in the United States of America
2 – BP – 12/31/09

[alien agent]
series

For all my White Meadows camp counselors—
though you never had campers like these.

—P.S.

To Mom and Dad, who paid for my education
and allowed me to pursue a career that really
didn't make much sense on paper. Thank you!

—M.G.

Prologue

Agent Sorn walked to a table in the Galactic Union headquarters cafeteria and plunked down her plate. The cafeteria's gurlg worms were never as crispy as her brood mother used to make them, but they would do. She'd just picked up an eating prong when she felt a buzzing vibration on her wrist that signaled an incoming call on her communicator band. She flipped up the two-way video screen and Chief Agent Zythis's face appeared in a fine haze of static. Even with the bad reception she could see he wasn't happy. All of his many eyes were frowning at several reports being held by different tentacles. She could see an info cube in yet another tentacle. This couldn't be good.

"Agent Sorn responding, sir," she spoke into the tiny communicator speaker.

As he looked up from the report, Chief Agent Zythis's multiple eyes zeroed in on her. "Agent Sorn," he said gravely. "You have a urgent new assignment."

Still tired from her recent assignment in Kwithtuth IV, she tried not to sigh. "Where to this time, sir?"

"A brief trip back to planet Earth. A crisis has arisen that our planted agent there needs to deal with."

"But, the boy's not ready yet!" she protested. "He only just learned of his alien origins—far earlier than we'd planned—and already he was nearly killed by Gnairt assassins."

Zythis sighed through his several mouths. "I know, but until the Galactic

Union invites Earth to join, he's the only near-native agent we have there, and you are his contact."

The tentacle holding the info cube came into focus. "I've already made you an appointment in the Physical Alteration Lab. I know you hate to change your lovely purple skin for the boring shades that Earth humans seem to go in for, but at least you can keep your white hair. This info cube will be waiting for you when you get there—it will tell you everything you need to know. Don't worry. It's a simple assignment. He'll be in no danger. We're counting on you, Sorn, don't let us down. Over and out."

His image faded from the screen, and Sorn angrily snapped the communicator band shut and started to prong some more gurlg worms. But she had lost her appetite. "A simple assignment," she muttered. "Ha! So far nothing about planet Earth has been simple."

CHAPTER ONE

CAMP TAKHAMAGAK

The summer wasn't even half through, and I thought it couldn't possibly get any weirder. How wrong could I be?

I'd begun the summer by learning that I, Zackary Gaither, wasn't even human. I'm really an alien agent, planted on Earth to carry out a big-time mission. It seems that there's something called the Galactic Union. It's an organization of planets, like a *really big* United Nations. Earth isn't part of the Union yet. I was placed here to grow up "human" and learn the planet's ways. Eventually, I'm to act as a go-between when the Galactic Union contacts Earth and offers to let the planet join. Sort of like an interplanetary ambassador.

This whole thing was news to me. I first found out about it when a couple of creepy alien guys tried to wipe me out. They were enemies of the Union, and they didn't want Earth joining up. So I had to be told about my mission way earlier than the Union planned. Talk about mind-blowing!

I was numb for a few weeks after learning it all, but it's odd how quickly you can get used to things. My family and friends still think I am human. My parents have always thought they'd adopted a regular human kid. And frankly, being a human kid was all I'd ever known. So after a while, I stopped feeling weird about it and slipped back into my ordinary summer life. I did a week of theater class at the Arts Center and started looking forward to a session of horseback riding at Camp Trailblazer.

That's when things started getting weird again.

A few days before I was scheduled to go to camp, I came back from an afternoon playing video games with my friend Ken.

I headed directly for the kitchen, but before I
even placed a hand on the refrigerator, my mom
came in from the dining room and waved a letter in front of me—a letter on Camp Trailblazer
stationery.

"Change of plans, Zack. It seems that they
signed up too many campers and are now randomly assigning some to other camps."

"Meaning me?" I asked, sinking into a kitch-
en chair. It wasn't just the riding I'd been
looking forward to. Ken and some of my other
friends were going to Camp Trailblazer too.

"Yes, but it looks like the camp they chose
for you is a great substitute. Camp Takhamasak
is a lot more expensive than we could usually
afford, but they're making up the difference.
And it's way off in the mountains."

She handed me a brochure. Dully I looked
at it. Mountains, trees, a lake, and no horses. Probably the biggest animals around would
be mosquitoes. The camp had three units
with majorly geeky names—Arts Angels, Nature
Nuts, and Sports Sprites. I'd been signed

up for Nature Nuts. Nice of them to give me a choice.

That evening my folks could see I was in a major funk, so they took me along with them to the county fair. Lots of fun if you like looking at pigs and visiting booths about fertilizer and tractor companies. I don't.

Mom and Dad had a shift volunteering at the Humane Society booth, so I just wandered. I consoled myself by guzzling greasy funnel cakes, pork barbecue, and root beer while I drifted through the various boring exhibit buildings.

Turning a corner in one, I almost collided with Melanie Steeples and a gaggle of her giggling friends. Melanie had played the part of Snow White in the production we did at the end of my summer theater class. She would have been better cast as the Wicked Queen. She *was* the queen of annoying, self-centered airheads. I'd played the Woodsman and had often been tempted to finish her off early with my ax.

"Look, it's the Woodsman," she exclaimed, setting off a round of giggles. "Sorry, I can't remember your real name."

"Zack," I growled.

"Right, Zack." Dramatically Melanie pointed at a bulletin board, jangling a wrist-full of bangles. "Come look at these pictures of the Fair Queen Candidates and tell us your choice."

Dutifully I looked at the ten photographs of beaming girls, most of whom looked like older clones of Melanie—bouncy blond hair, fake smiles, heavy makeup. I deliberately pointed to the least attractive of them.

"You're hopeless!" More giggles from Melanie's fan club. "When I'm old enough, I'm *definitely* going to be Fair Queen. It's an important career step."

At theater class, we'd heard endlessly about her career plan which, through various unlikely moves, ended with her as a big Hollywood star.

As she and her friends went back to jabbering, I glowered at the queen candidates. They might all have career plans as unrealistic as Melanie's, but at least they had some choices. I apparently had no more choice in careers than I had in summer camps. What do you want to be when you grow up, Zack? An alien agent? Right.

Now totally ignored by Melanie's gang, I slipped away from the exhibit buildings and drifted toward the amusement park. I figured the carnival music, swirling lights, and smell of cotton candy ought to cheer me up. They didn't much, but I had enough money for maybe one ride. After my greasy meal, my stomach didn't feel up to anything fast. But the Ferris wheel was really tall, and I remembered you could get a great view from the top.

As I got in line, Melanie and her gang giggled past me, loudly saying something about skipping the "baby rides." Well, at least I had enough choices left in life to choose a cool view rather than throwing up.

When I reached the head of the line, I would

have been willing to share a car, but the smoochy couple ahead of me didn't look like they wanted company. The fat lady and kid behind me wouldn't have had room, so I got into the swinging seat by myself. The attendant was just lowering the bar when a white-haired woman bustled up and cried, "Zack, dear! What a wonderful chance to talk with my favorite nephew. We'll share!"

I was too startled to object. She sat beside me, the bar clanked down, and we jerked forward and off the ground. I stared at my companion. I do have a pushy aunt. But this wasn't her. This was Sorn, the white-haired alien lady who'd helped save me from the creepy aliens a couple months ago.

"Sorry to butt in, Zack, but I need to talk with you alone. An unexpected crisis has come up on this planet, and the Galactic Union simply doesn't have enough operatives around to handle it. Even though you're not trained yet, you're our only agent on Earth. I'm afraid we'll have to call on you for help."

My stomach felt like I'd gone on one of those really fast rides after all.

"What kind of crisis?" I managed to say.

"The Gnairt again." I felt even sicker, remembering the fat, bald, human-looking guys who had tried to kill me. They'd found out I was the planted Galactic Union agent and didn't want me to mess up their own plans for the planet. "Not the same ones, of course," she said quickly. "We dealt with them. These are Duthwi-egg smugglers. And they could cause a planetwide disaster."

I stared at her. White hair or not, nothing about Sorn looked soft and grandmotherly. "Egg smuggling? Doesn't sound too disastrous to me."

She fixed me with her very intense, almost purple gaze. "These Gnairt were smuggling a valuable shipload of Duthwi eggs across this sector when a Galactic Patrol ship gave chase. They ducked into your solar system, dumping their cargo on Earth so they wouldn't be caught with the evidence."

"So, what's the problem. The smugglers got away?"

"For the time being. But the real problem is that we can't have Duthwi eggs hatching on Earth. Not only could they create an environmental disaster, but they look very alien and that could freak your natives out. We don't want that kind of negative attitude toward aliens a few years before the Galactic Union establishes contact with Earth."

"So why don't you just go and pick up these eggs?"

"We would if we had the manpower. But I need to be elsewhere, and we've only been able to assign one Galactic Patrol Cadet to the job. She'll need someone familiar with native culture to help her."

I glanced away, realizing vaguely that the Ferris wheel had already gone around once without me noticing the view. "But this is crazy! Kids on Earth can't just take off on secret missions without adults asking questions and probably saying no."

"We've taken care of that. You'll be leaving shortly for a site near where we believe the Duthwi eggs were dumped, somewhere just east of Lake Takhamasak. Our Cadet will meet you there with further details."

Suddenly I felt like I'd been dumped out of the Ferris wheel. "Wait a minute! *You* had me turned down by Camp Trailblazer and sent to Camp Takhamasak instead!"

"Rather clever, I thought, for such short notice."

"But it's not fair! I didn't choose to . . . "

She fixed me again with those amethyst eyes. "Zack, few of us of whatever species have complete free choice over our lives. You can choose not to help, if you want, but I imagine that after living on this planet all your life, you might care enough about it to choose saving it from harm."

I swallowed like I was fighting motion sickness. She had me there. Maybe I *was* an alien, but I didn't feel like one. Earth was my home, and if I could keep some nasty aliens from messing it up, I guess I had to try.

"Right," I muttered. "So how do I recognize this Galactic Patrol Cadet, and what do Duthwi eggs look like anyway, and what do I do with them if I find them?"

She smiled. "Our Cadet will explain everything. Her name is Itl Vraj Boynyo Tg. I'd help if I could, but tomorrow I'm supposed to be light-years from here. I have faith in you though, Zack. I wish things hadn't started for you so early. We really had hoped to give you more time just to grow up. But this is your job. You'll be good at it."

With a swing and a bump, our chair reached the bottom and stopped. The bar lifted, and I stepped off, dazed. Sorn patted my arm and disappeared into the crowd.

I blinked. I'd gone on an entire Ferris wheel ride and hadn't seen a thing. But just the same, my world had been turned totally upside down.

CHAPTER TWO

I didn't have long to get used to this secret mission thing. James Bond from outer
space. None of it seemed like *me*. But two
days later, I was standing in front of the school
where a bus would be picking up kids for Camp
Takhamasak.

Those two days, though, had been long
enough for me to decide that if I was going to
give up an ordinary summer for this crazy job,
I might as well do it right. I'd look for their
stupid lost eggs and hope that after that these
Galactic Union people or whatever would leave
me alone for a few years.

And hey, I told myself as I hauled my bulging pack from my mom's car, how hard could

this be? I'd had years of experience looking for Easter eggs. Around our house, the Easter Bunny, otherwise known as my dad, was fiendishly clever at hiding them. Besides, there'd be this alien Cadet with the unpronounceable name to help.

So who was this person? "She," Sorn had said. I looked around at the other kids gathered at the curb. Some had parents hovering embarrassingly around, but most, like my Mom, were waiting properly in their cars. I didn't recognize most of the kids, but at the end of the crowd, dribbling a basketball, was Scott Turner, that jock jerk from my school. True to form, he had swarms of girls hanging around him. I groaned. One of them was Melanie the airhead. Well, *she* certainly wouldn't be the Galactic Cadet in disguise.

I felt a tug on my jacket. "Hello, Woodsman. Remember me?" I looked down at a girl a couple years younger than me, short and plump with stringy brown hair and very wide eyes. "I'm Bashful."

I remembered, and she certainly was—having been typecast as Bashful the Dwarf in our Snow White play. Why any parents would send someone that shy to an acting class, I couldn't imagine. Whenever she got up in front of people, her words totally dried up. Now, though, she was chattering nervously. "My real name's Opal, and I remember that you're Zack. I didn't really want to go to this camp. I get awfully homesick, but here I am. You're the only person I know here except for Snow White over there. I bet you're signed up for the Arts Angels unit. You're such a good actor."

"Actually, I'm in Nature Nuts," I managed to slip in.

Her eyes practically shone. "So am I!"

Just then a big yellow bus rumbled up. In the jostling crowd, I tried to edge away from my young admirer. It didn't work. I'd no sooner found a seat than Opal plunked down beside me. After tearfully waving to someone outside the window, she began to chatter about her hamster and her seashell collection. I grunted a few times in reply and sank into my own thoughts.

Not generally pleasant thoughts.

These Galactic Union aliens really couldn't have much of a clue about Earth. They seemed to think that sending me somewhere near those eggs would be enough. But at a summer camp for human kids, you can't just wander off looking for things whenever you want. There are schedules, and adults are watching you. If you do something really dumb, they call your parents and send you home. I guess that's one reason they needed me. I'd certainly have some major briefing to do for their secret agent.

But first I'd have to find her. I scanned the girls on the bus, and then with a start I looked down at Opal. She was going on about her science experiments in school.

"Do you know anything about Duthwi eggs?" I asked innocently.

The blank look she gave was either real or better acting than she'd done during the whole theater class. "No, but I used duck eggs in one experiment." As she chattered on about that, I realized that the alien Cadet probably wasn't a camper but might be a counselor. So I gave up searching and just stared out the window, watching the trees change from the round lollipop types that little kids like to draw to ones more like Christmas trees without lights. And then I dozed.

Hours later, the bus left the highway for a dirt road that jolted upward through miles of dark woods. The trees were crammed close together, and the dim space under them was filled with bushes and fallen logs. How could anyone find eggs scattered through country like this?

Finally we rumbled up to some wooden buildings, and I peered through the bus's dusty window at the people waiting for us. No one was acting like "It's me, I'm the alien." Maybe I should be carrying a sign like people do when they are meeting someone they don't know at an airport. "Secret Alien Agent" or something.

Once off the bus, we were all trooped to the smelly latrines, then to a big meeting with all the campers. Everyone sat on their luggage in a big open space around a tall flagpole. The counselors told us the camp rules and schedule and gave out cabin assignments. I was sure glad Opal was a girl and would finally have to let go of me. But she didn't seem too happy when she learned who her cabinmates were— Melanie and blond twins, Bessy and Jessy, who looked and acted like cheerleaders. I couldn't really blame her.

My own assignment wasn't great. A couple of brothers from another school, Ramon and Carlos, seemed OK. But then there was Scott, the All-American Sports Hero. Oh well, I reminded myself, I wasn't here to have a good time but to do a job.

Like all the others, our cabin was a rustic log box that looked like Abe Lincoln could have lived there. At least I managed to snag a top bunk. The brothers fought over who got the other top bunk, but Scott in his usual take-charge way settled the matter by grabbing it himself. And the brothers seemed to love him for it. They suffered from major hero-worship. Good thing all three of my cabinmates were in Sports Sprites so I wouldn't have to deal with them much.

The only furniture besides the beds were four small cupboards for storing our stuff. We'd just started unpacking when the lunch gong sounded. Before joining the flow to the dining hall, I headed up the pinecone-lined path to the nearest latrine. It was dark inside the little wooden building and eye-wateringly smelly. Trying to hold my breath, I stepped in. I'd no sooner shut the door than I heard a scratching on the walls—the outside of the walls, fortunately, but it became louder. Bears? Could bears break through wooden planks?

Then came a harsh whisper. "Follow the path up the hill and meet me at the lone tree."

I let out my breath. Not bears. The Cadet.

"When?" I asked.

"Whenever you can break away from the group."

As soon as I'd finished in the latrine, I ran behind the building but couldn't see anything. At least I'd made contact. I would try to slip away after lunch.

The dining hall was a big open-sided shed, like a huge picnic shelter with heavy log pillars holding up the roof. Long tables and benches were lined up on a concrete slab. After filing through the serving line, we sat down to eat tomato soup and greasy grilled cheese sandwiches. Then the counselors had us play get-acquainted games and sing songs.

My mind wasn't on any of it. I kept looking around at the counselors, the cooks, and even the janitors, wondering who the alien was. A female with a harsh voice was all I knew.

After lunch, I saw Opal outside the dining hall, shyly standing alone. Before I could slip away, she latched onto me and began complaining about her cabinmates. "All they do is talk about cheerleading and becoming movie stars or dancers. I'm a klutz at all that.

They don't talk about animals or rocks or anything outdoorsy. I wish you were a girl so I could be your cabinmate."

I silently thanked heaven that I wasn't, said something dippy about how she'd probably get to like them once she knew them better, then slipped off in the direction of the boys' cabins. What I'd just told her was probably good advice that I should try to apply to myself and my own cabinmates. But frankly, making friends wasn't what I needed to be focusing on now. I had an assignment to get through.

Once most people had returned to their cabins for what was billed as "rest time," I strolled instead toward the latrine, then passed by its stinky island, and continued up the hill. After a while, a faint path left the trees and continued through a stretch of dry grass to an ancient, gnarled pine tree. There was no one around. I sat at the base of the tree, wishing I could remember the Cadet's name so I could call her.

The sun was warm. Leaning against the rough trunk, I looked sleepily around at the rocks poking through the thin soil. On one, a lizard sat sunning himself, unmoving except for the tiny rise and fall of his jeweled sides. Insects whirred and birds chirped.

With a start I opened my eyes, realizing I'd fallen asleep. It couldn't have been for long. The lizard was still there.

I gasped. No way was that the same lizard! It was bigger, much bigger. I jumped up and stared. It looked like something from a dinosaur movie. A velociraptor!

It was six feet away, and I was staring right into its eyes. Yellow, beady eyes.

"Zackary Gaither," it hissed. "Galactic Agents do not sleep on duty!"

CHapter Three

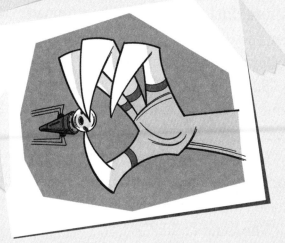

I stared at the Hollywood horror in front of me. My legs tensed, but I forced myself to stay. This was my partner!

Swallowing, I croaked, "Fine, but I'm just the local help. You're . . . what was your name again?"

"Itl Vraj Boynyo Tg." The creature's toothy mouth twitched in an unmistakable sneer. "Obviously that's beyond you. Use Vraj."

"Right. I'm Zack." I tried not to stare at those teeth and claws. I knew I shouldn't be surprised that some aliens would look . . . really *alien*. It's just that most of those I'd met before, including me, looked human. No wonder this one needed some help. She certainly couldn't pass as a native.

"So what do we do now?" I said, trying to sound like I talked to velociraptor look-alikes every day.

"What I've been doing for two days—looking for Duthwi eggs. And I could finish this job by myself if it weren't for the time factor."

"The time factor?"

With a gargling growl, she flung up her short arms. "Put in this translator. Speaking your language hurts worse than having teeth pulled."

She reached into a shoulder bag and held up a little black thing that looked like a metal spider. Then she jammed it into my ear. I stumbled back against the tree. Talk about pain! It felt like someone had attacked my ear with a heavy-duty staple gun. But before I could scream, the pain had dropped to a low throb. Hesitantly, I poked a finger into my ear. I couldn't feel any bump. Had the thing gone right inside?

She was talking again. "The more light that Duthwi eggs are exposed to, the sooner they hatch." Now I could hear growly sounds underlying echoey English. I tried to concentrate on the words instead of my sore ear.

"But we don't know when this batch was laid," she said, "so we don't know how long we have."

"Where do we look?" I asked and was suddenly unsure what language I'd said that in. My throat hurt like I'd swallowed a cactus. Was I actually speaking her language? Cool. This gizmo in my ear could be a big help in my Spanish class.

In any case, she'd clearly understood me. "The smugglers dumped them in a rocky ravine on the other side of this hill." She jabbed a clawed finger toward the north. At least that sounded close.

"So they should be pretty easy to collect," I suggested. She snorted, and I half expected to see smoke billow from her nostrils. "You haven't seen a Duthwi egg, have you?"

She reached into a large bag and thrust something round into my hand. It was shaped like a large potato with a rough, gray-brown surface. Basically it looked like a rock, but it felt a lot lighter than a rock that size should feel.

"What's worse," she said, "is that no two are exactly alike. I have a device that detects them, but it only works when I'm already close. In two days, I've only found seven."

"How many were there to start with?"

"One hundred."

Ninety-three rocklike things to find in a ravine full of rocks. I groaned. "What's so special about these things that anyone would bother smuggling them anyway?"

Her sneer exposed an alarming number of teeth. I hoped Cadets weren't allowed to eat their partners. "You certainly are ignorant. Duthwi are among the most prized hunting prey in the galaxy. They are fast and challenging to hit. And they are absolutely delicious to eat."

She grinned. Don't look at her teeth, I told myself. Look at her... skin. A pebbly, yellow-green, it looked slick and hard as china—not that anyone would want a china figurine anything like Vraj.

Snatching the egg back, she continued. "They're an endangered species because so many other species hunt them. Those Gnairt were taking them to an illegal hunting reserve somewhere in this sector. Once we round up the eggs, the Patrol will send a ship to return them to their home world. They're too dangerous to leave here."

How dangerous? I added that to the list of questions I didn't have time to ask. I needed to get back. "OK, I'll help you tonight. It's hard for me to get away during the day, and you shouldn't risk being out in the daylight in case anyone sees you."

She growled. "Yes. A young native saw me yesterday and made an unimaginable fuss."

I *could* imagine. Good thing kids from that last session had already left. Luckily, no one would believe a kid saying they'd seen a dinosaur anyway. "I'll meet you by this tree once everyone's asleep."

"Don't dawdle. Your schedule is slowing my mission enough."

What a charmer, I thought as I headed back to the cabin. Was this one a particular jerk, or was her whole species like her? I sighed. At the rate Vraj had been collecting eggs, it would take every night this session to find them all. Lots of sleep was obviously not in my future.

As I trudged past the outhouse, something leapt at me. I stifled a yelp. "Opal! What are you doing here?"

"And what are you doing chatting with monsters? What *was* that thing?"

Trouble. I'd been warned that one of my main duties was to keep the existence of aliens an absolute secret. I had to think fast.

"What do you think it was?"

"Well, it *looked* like a dinosaur, but I'm not that stupid."

"Oh, but it *is* a dinosaur." I looked around

theatrically. "This is a really big secret. You can't tell anyone."

Her eyes were enormous. "I promise. A real dinosaur? But how..."

"My dad's a scientist. He learned that not all dinosaurs became extinct. Some evolved into intelligent creatures, but they hide from humans so that we don't put them in zoos. This one needs our help, that's all."

"Cool! Can I help too?"

I tried not to groan. A lot of good it would do to say no. She'd just tag along anyway. "OK. I'll meet you here after lights-out. *If* we think we can trust you, you can help."

"Oh yes, you can trust me!"

I looked her in the eye. "I hope so, because even evolved dinosaurs aren't always friendly—especially ones with big teeth."

Opal went pale as a marshmallow but quavered, "Got it. Absolute secret."

"Good. Now let's get back before we're both in trouble."

I caught some trouble anyway when I entered

my cabin. "Didn't you hear the rules?" Scott snapped. "At rest time we're supposed to be in our cabins."

"Well, I am *now*," I said, climbing to my bunk. "I had to cheer up a younger camper who was majorly homesick." The other three made snide comments but went back to reading their sports magazines. I laid on my bunk, worrying about a supposedly simple assignment that had turned out to be full of camouflaged eggs, an alien dinosaur, and a really inconvenient witness. Finally, a gong called us all to our units.

Nature Nuts House was a small log building next to an open-sided shelter like a smaller version of the dining hall. A half-dozen tables and benches filled the open space. I sat at one randomly then glanced up to see Opal sliding onto the bench across from me, looking like she would burst with our secret. She'd never make a spy.

Muskrat, the chief Nature Nuts counselor, began talking about the wonders of nature we'd discover: animals, trees, insects, birds, wild-flowers, and weather. And we'd all do an individual project.

I wasn't paying much attention until Opal leaned forward and whispered loudly, "I'll do my project on dinosaurs!"

"A lovely idea," Muskrat said, overhearing, "but let's confine our projects to parts of nature we can actually see."

At that Opal giggled and kicked me under the table. I glowered menacingly at her, wishing I had Vraj's teeth to back it up.

The afternoon was spent in a meadow south of camp looking at wildflowers. Thrilling, I'm sure, but I kept my eyes open for Duthwi eggs. All of the rocks I picked up were heavy like real rocks. Muskrat noticed my rock fixation.

"Maybe you'd like your special project to be about rocks, Zack," she said brightly.

I nodded glumly. I had enough special projects already.

The rest of the day went by in a blur. More

nature stuff, dinner, a campfire with songs and marshmallows. Mostly my mind was on how to make my non-extinct dinosaur story more convincing for Opal while not ticking off Vraj that I'd involved a clueless native.

Back in our cabin, Ramon, Carlos, and Scott all started chattering about the endurance course they were going to run. I slipped under my covers, hoping nobody noticed I was fully dressed, and pretended to fall asleep. Eventually the others did for real, and I lay there thinking about how to get down from my bunk without shaking the creaky bed and waking someone up.

I could always say I had to go to the latrine, but if I did that every night they might get suspicious. But suspicious of what? That I was a recovering bed wetter? That I was really a vampire who slipped out at night to suck blood? No, a vampire could just turn into a bat and fly off without creaking anything. OK, so not a vampire. An alien.

I smiled a little at that. There *were* those

alien powers I'd discovered earlier. Since then I'd tried not to think about them, because they freaked me out. Actually the climbing hadn't been too scary, but what freaked me out was that it *didn't* scare me. It came perfectly naturally. Not for the first time, I wondered what my real species was like. I shrugged the thought away. Basically I was human—with just a few odd additions.

Quietly, I slipped to the foot of my bunk where it butted against a wall. Trying to keep my mind blank, I grabbed the rough logs and scrambled down like Lizardman.

I left the cabin with everyone still asleep, then hurried toward the latrine. Smell hung around the place like a cloud, but Opal wasn't there yet. I hoped maybe she'd forgotten, but soon I heard her crunching up the path. Definitely not spy material.

She jumped when I stepped out of the shadows, but she recovered quickly and said, "OK, Zack, tell me what your friend needs help with."

I had my story ready. "Like I said, these evolved dinosaurs stay away from humans, except for people they trust, like my dad and me. This one was in charge of moving a nursery of dinosaur eggs away from where people were building new houses. But there was an accident, and the eggs spilled over a mountainside near here. So my friend needs help collecting them.

"Wow!" Opal was silent a moment. "You can talk with her?"

I nodded. My ear still hurt from the translator. "Dad taught me their language. I'll have to translate for you." At least Opal wouldn't be able to hear what that nasty-tempered alien was really saying.

"Come on," I said as I headed off through the dark and rather spooky forest. Shadows moved jaggedly in the wind, and the only sounds were creaking branches and hissing pine needles. "Maybe she's there already," I said, trying to hurry Opal along. "Dinosaurs are short tempered. They don't like to be kept waiting."

The same could be said for grouchy aliens, but I kept that to myself.

But Vraj wasn't there. We were alone on the open hillside except for the big tree, rustling night creatures, and a whole lot of stars overhead.

"Look, there's Andromeda!" Opal said.

My head swiveled around. Not another camper! Then I noticed Opal was pointing into the sky.

"You hardly ever get to see her in a city. Too much light. And there's Pegasus above her, that big square."

Constellations. Actually, I kind of wished I knew something about them, since I apparently came from out there somewhere. Maybe Opal could ...

My thoughts were snapped back to earth by a cracking twig. Vraj bounded up to us, scales glinting in the starlight. Opal shrank back against me.

"What's this?" the alien growled in her language.

"Opal saw you, Vraj," I said in English, using what I hoped was a calm, soothing voice. "And she wants to help. I explained how you are an *evolved dinosaur* hiding from humans and that you lost a bunch of *dinosaur* eggs and need help finding them."

Vraj's face crinkled into an expression I was glad I couldn't read. "This infant thinks I'm an extinct primitive reptile?" Her snarl was untranslatable. "Well, what's done is done. But she'd better keep quiet about this."

"Opal's promised not to say a word," I said loudly.

"Right," Opal quavered timidly from behind me. I was glad she was only getting my end of the conversation. "I can keep secrets."

Vraj growled at me. "She'd better. Remember, neither of us can afford to have this mission fail."

Though I still didn't know exactly what the danger was, Sorn had made it clear these Duthwi were a threat to Earth. Was Vraj so uptight about the mission because she was a

Cadet trying to prove herself? Maybe this was her first mission. If she was just a kid, I'd hate to meet her parents.

Vraj held out an egg. "All right. This is what we're looking for. Not easy on a rocky hillside in the dark."

I looked at the egg clutched in her claw. "But it helps that it glows."

"Glows?" Vraj growled.

Mistake. *I* could see the glow, but apparently Vraj's kind of alien couldn't. I didn't want Opal to catch on that I had special alien powers. "Eh . . . maybe it's just reflecting starlight."

"No, it's glowing all right," Opal chirped. "These should be as easy to find as giant glowworms."

I relaxed. It seemed that humans and my own species could both see the glow, but Vraj's beady yellow eyes couldn't. The Cadet grunted with annoyance and turned to go uphill. She moved ahead in quick jerky steps, her tail sweeping back and forth. I guess, all told, I was lucky to get this sort of alien for a partner. Something that looked like a badly animated movie dinosaur was still easier to explain to Opal than some green alien with three heads.

Through the misty starlight, Vraj led us over the crest of a ridge and onto a steep hillside bare of everything but rocks. Zillions of rocks. Glow or not, it wasn't going to be easy to find those eggs. And if we didn't find them soon, two mismatched alien kids—and maybe this whole planet—could be in big trouble.

CHAPTER FOUR

It was the weirdest egg hunt I'd ever been on. After long hours of scrabbling in the dark, we were tired and cold, and our eyes ached. All we had to show for it were nine more eggs. Nine plus Vraj's seven left eighty-four more eggs to find.

The sky was paling to gray when Opal and I slipped back into our cabins. It seemed like the wake-up gong sounded only seconds after I'd crawled into bed. But by then it was fully light, and everyone was bustling around, excited about the first full day of camp. As for me, I almost fell asleep at breakfast and nearly drowned in my pancake syrup.

After breakfast, I blearily noticed that Melanie had cornered Opal between the dining hall and the nurse's cabin and was apparently making her cry. I told myself to ignore it, but nobody deserves to be bullied, not even little pests like Opal. And with Opal holding that big secret, I figured I'd better check things out.

"So who's your boyfriend?" Melanie was saying as I walked closer. "Tell me, or I'll tell the counselors I saw you sneak out last night to meet a boy."

"I didn't," Opal sobbed. "I don't have a boyfriend."

Melanie had backed Opal against a tree and was smirking down at her. Angrily, I stepped up to them. "Hey, leave the kid alone," I said. "Don't you have some artsy showing off to do?"

Melanie spluttered. Then suddenly a nasty glint came into her eye. "It was *you*, wasn't it? The guy was tall and dark haired. I saw that when they came back."

Opal started to protest, but I jumped in. "Melanie, who would have guessed you have such a dirty mind? If you must know, we're planning our Nature Nuts project. We want to lead a nighttime hike, but we need to figure out where to go."

Opal, eyes big and teary, nodded earnestly.

Melanie sneered. "You expect me to believe that?"

I shrugged. "Who cares what you believe? But when we get the hike planned, Arts Farts and Sports Dorks will *not* be invited."

As we split up, Opal gave me the thumbs up, followed by what looked like dinosaur claws. When it came to keeping a secret, that kid was a time bomb.

Still, when we got to Nature Nuts that morning, I had an idea churning. As Opal and I settled onto a bench, I tried it on Muskrat. "Opal and I have a great project idea, and it could involve other people's projects too. A nighttime hike. Chelsea could do her bird-call project with owls, and Opal could point out constellations and tell their stories."

I talked right over Opal's squeaking protest. "And I could do a thing about rocks. My dad says there's a special type of rock on a hillside near here. They sort of glow in the dark, so searching for them would be perfect for a nighttime hike."

Suddenly catching on, Opal stifled a giggle. Muskrat beamed. "Wonderful. We counselors were thinking of a nighttime hike, but we never knew about the rocks. Nothing's scheduled for tomorrow night. How about holding it then?"

"But I can't talk in front of people about constellations," Opal whispered after Muskrat had gone.

"Of course you can. You know your stuff, and this will make good our excuse to Melanie. Plus it will give us an army to look for Vraj's eggs."

Nature Nuts spent the afternoon looking for animal tracks on the muddy edge of a swamp. Mostly that meant dodging mosquitoes and water snakes. Beyond the reeds, we could hear the Sports Sprites having fun canoeing on Lake Takhamasak. I had to keep telling myself I was *not* at this camp to have fun. Still, canoeing appealed a bit more to me than tracking toads in a swamp.

That night I convinced Opal to stay in her cabin so Melanie wouldn't get all suspicious again. I sneaked out to the lone pine to tell Vraj our plans. The scaly alien guilt-tripped me into looking for eggs for a few hours, bringing our total number of eggs needed down to eighty-one. Hopefully reinforcements would help.

At breakfast the next day, the nature counselors announced that our group would go on an overnight nature hike that evening. We spent much of that day planning for the excursion. After dinner, the Nature Nuts shouldered packs and sleeping bags and headed for the hill with the lone pine, the place that Opal and I had suggested. Not much of a trek from a hiking point of view, but it nicely fit the counselors' idea of experiencing nature at night.

Chelsea did her owl talk, and a real owl even answered her feeble imitations. A kid named Walt talked about nighttime animals like raccoons, possums, and skunks. There were lots of skunk jokes after that, but I was more worried about seeing dinosaurs at night. I had warned Vraj to stay out of sight, but she didn't seem to take orders well from a near native.

Next was Opal's turn. Muskrat practically had to drag her from behind the pine tree to get her to stand in front of the group. Mechanically Opal began pointing out constellations and mumbling the names that are attached to each group of stars. But when someone asked her about the names, Opal started telling the Greek myths about each constellation. By the time she got to the story of Andromeda, she was really into it, and her shyness evaporated.

"This one's got a really cool myth," she said enthusiastically. "This queen, named Cassiopeia, brags that her daughter, Andromeda, is prettier than the sea god Neptune's daughters. Neptune gets mad and sends Draco the Sea Monster to destroy the town. Well, Andromeda's dad, King Cepheus, chains Andromeda to a rock so Draco will eat her instead. (Thanks, Dad.)" The kids laughed at that, and Opal beamed.

"So meanwhile," she continued, "somewhere else in Greece, a hero named Perseus has just killed the Gorgon, a lady with snakes for hair who is so ugly that people turn to stone just looking at her. He flies by on his winged horse, Pegasus, turns Draco to stone with the Gorgon's head, and then flies off with Andromeda to live happily ever after."

All those characters were supposed to be seen in the constellations. Those ancient Greeks must have had pretty good imaginations to connect a bunch of scattered stars into those pictures. I wondered suddenly if people on the planet I came from connected stars into different constellations. I had to drop that train of thought as Opal finished her talk. Everyone applauded, and she blushed a bright, happy red.

It was my turn next, but the campers were getting pretty restless, so I raised my voice and threw my arms around like I was on stage.

"Listen up, Nature Nuts! Now comes the exciting Magic Stone Quest. Duthwite is a rare rock that can only be found near here. We're going out and looking for it!"

"Looking for rocks at night?" some kid called. "Give us a break!"

"Ah, that's the best time to find Duthwite. By day, it looks like this." I held up one egg Vraj had lent me and shone my flashlight on it. It looked like a dirty potato.

"So it's a rock. Big deal," that kid said.

"But at night, it looks like this!" I switched off my flashlight. The "rock" glowed a spooky blue-green.

"Oooo," everyone said.

"Now, we're going to look for them. The person who finds the most wins this huge bag of candy!"

I held up the bag my mom had given me to share with my cabinmates. My particular cabinmates hadn't inspired me to share much, but this was a good cause.

We all trooped over the ridge into the rocky valley, twenty-five kids and three counselors. This army of Nature Nuts spread over the hillside and soon began finding "Duthwite." Even the counselors were having too much fun to call it quits. But after a couple of hours, the finds became fewer and the younger kids were tiring, so we trooped back to our hillside camp. After the counselors checked each kid's take, the prize went to a shy kid named Ted who suddenly had a lot of friends.

Once the campfire was going, the others roasted marshmallows and sang songs while I counted the eggs and stuffed them into sacks. Eighty exactly. We'd only missed one! Vraj could find that one on her own. As for me, it was Mission Accomplished.

After everyone had quieted down and crawled into their sleeping bags, I looked up at the countless stars spangling overhead. A shooting star streaked silently across the others, disappearing behind the trees. Out there, some people were wondering if a couple of alien agents down here were doing their job. And we had! Vraj would get the eggs out of here, the mysterious danger they posed to Earth would be gone, and aliens would leave me alone for a while. Maybe I could even start enjoying this camp, horses or not.

Which goes to show that when things seem too good to be true, they usually are.

CHAPTER FIVE

Back at camp the next morning, I stored the sacks of "Duthwite" in a closet at Nature Nuts House, and that night I reported briefly to Vraj. She planned to search that night for the last egg, collect the others, and leave Earth.

So the following morning, when Muskrat reported anxiously that someone had stolen my Duthwite, I was hardly surprised, though the way the closet door had been smashed in just confirmed that Vraj was an inconsiderate, or at least impatient, jerk. But anyway, all that was behind me now, so I was determined to focus on actually being at camp.

Our activity that morning had us sitting at the tables by the Nature Nuts House and making baskets from reeds we'd collected in the swamp. Mine looked like a nest that birds had rejected. Opal was actually sitting with other friends she'd been making. I was happy to be sitting by myself at a table by the edge of the woods.

When I came back to the table from getting more reeds, another kid had joined me. His basket looked pretty good, but I couldn't see his face under his pulled down hat. His thin fingers were weaving reeds like lightning. Thin fingers with long claws.

"Vraj?" I whispered, peering under the hat. "I thought you'd be gone by now!" She grimaced with all her teeth. The shirt fit oddly and her tail must have been tucked into the baggy pants.

Sticking her mouth frighteningly close, she hissed. "The Gnairt are back. They stole all

the eggs you found from your Nature Nuts closet and hauled them somewhere. Now, I've got
to find them again! *If* I need your help, I'll tap
at your window tonight. Those thieving Gnairt
probably won't leave without the eggs I found
earlier, and *mine* are well hidden."

I would have been annoyed at that jab if I
hadn't been so freaked at the idea of creepy
Gnairt being around.

"So how come your Galactic Patrol didn't
keep the Gnairt away?"

She snorted. "Patrol ships are spread thin
just now. Looks like we're on our own here."
If the translator got it right, she sounded a
little scared.

"Alert that Opal person too," she continued. "Much as I hate to say it, we may need
her help. Things are getting tricky, even for a
trained professional like me."

Trained indeed. She was just a kid getting
training on the job. Like me.

Vraj completed her basket and examined it
from several angles. Tucking it under her little

arm, she disappeared into the woods. The counselors never noticed the brief appearance of a new camper, though I wondered which kid would soon be reporting missing clothes.

At lunch I told Opal about the mysterious basket maker, and she was delighted about maybe having another adventure with her dinosaur friend. I wasn't. I'd had enough adventures with aliens for one year. But that night, I lulled myself to sleep with the thought that "experienced professional Vraj" could probably handle this herself, and I'd seen the last of her. Dream on.

A tapping noise—it sounded like a branch blowing against the glass—pulled me from sleep. There were no trees near that window. I scrambled down the log wall, pulled on clothes as quietly as I could, and slipped outside.

Two figures waited in the tree shadows cast by a bright half moon. "I've found the Gnairt's camp," Vraj whispered harshly. "They probably don't know they're dealing with an official of the Galactic Patrol, but I may need some backup in the rescue."

Opal was jumping around, wanting to know what the "dinosaur" said. I only changed it a little. "She says she may need our help rescuing the eggs from her enemies." I hoped that Opal would never actually meet those enemies. Gnairt might be sort of human looking, but based on personal experience, I knew they are definitely more dangerous than most of the dinosaurs that ever lived.

Vraj was already trotting off into the shadowy trees. Opal and I hurried, trying to catch up. I wondered if all of Vraj's people were this snotty or if it was only the cocky kids trying to prove how great they are.

We'd almost lost sight of Vraj when a voice came from the shadows right beside us. "Going somewhere, little lovers?"

We spun around. Two people stood there, one cabinmate for each of us—Scott and Melanie, both looking smug.

"Can't think of a more unlikely couple,"

Melanie said. "But isn't tapping on windows awfully old-fashioned?"

"Hey, it's not what you think," Opal protested.

"No," Scott offered. "Instead of going off to smooch in the woods, it's some science experiment. Forget it. You've already used up that excuse."

Opal was spluttering into a story, but I trusted my imagination more than hers. "It's not an experiment, it's a rescue. We found out who stole the Duthwite and we're going to get it back."

"Who'd want a bunch of old rocks?" Melanie laughed.

"What do you know?" Opal piped up. "You didn't see them."

"Right," I added. "They're rare glow-in-the-dark rocks. Rock dealers would pay lots for them."

Scott snorted. "So a couple of clueless kids confront big bad rock robbers. That's a weak TV plot."

"Sorry, but it's true." Then I smiled. "You can come and watch if you'd like. But maybe you ought to get back to your cabins before people start thinking *you two* are secret night-time lovers."

As both bubbled protest, I headed into the trees. "Come on, Opal, the trail's getting cold."

When I turned to check, we weren't being followed. But we had also lost our guide. After stumbling along for a while, we finally saw her waiting in a patch of watery moonlight, tail twitching impatiently.

"About time you shook those two. I don't need any more native help." She turned and jogged off again with us straggling behind. After what seemed like miles, she stopped at the top of a ridge.

"The Gnairt are camped down there. I listened in on them, and their plans have changed—for the worse. Instead of leaving with the eggs, they want to let them hatch here. Then they'll bring in rich hunters, using Earth's natural wildlife as an added hunting attraction."

"But that could . . . " I was struggling to find a way to say things so that Opal, who was understanding only my part of the conversation, wouldn't catch on to the truth.

Vraj continued through my translator. "That could devastate Earth, what with hatched Duthwi flying everywhere and alien hunters swarming about shooting every animal they see. It would totally destroy the Galactic Union's approach to bringing in new planets gradually. Your natives would hate aliens after that."

I felt sick and chilled, as if I'd chugged down too much ice water. The worst part was that so much depended on the three of us. Laughable— if it wasn't so scary.

"What's she saying?" Opal squeaked.

"Er . . . mainly she's cussing out the egg stealers. They're camped down there."

Creeping slowly to the crest of the ridge, we peered down through a screen of bushes. Nestled among trees below was what looked like a dome tent glowing with lantern light.

It was probably more high-tech than that, but for Opal's sake I was glad it looked so Earthly.

"They have the eggs in there with them," Vraj whispered. "We need to get the Gnairt away long enough to steal back the sacks. If I go down the valley a little way and create a diversion, you two could snatch the eggs."

I explained the plan to Opal. She liked it— better than I did. I knew these weren't bad guys trying to make a buck stealing glowing rocks. They were creepy aliens who packed some nasty weapons. But there didn't seem to be a lot of choices.

Vraj slipped off through the bushes and was soon out of sight. Lying on our stomachs on the damp mossy ground, Opal and I watched the tent. She tried to ask me more about evolved dinosaurs, but I shushed her. I doubted we could be heard from here, but my brain was tired of making up stuff.

The chugging and peeping of night creatures suddenly hushed. A new noise took over. It sounded like several people screaming at the tops of their lungs. Then they came crashing through bushes at the lower end of the ravine.

"Help! Eeeek! A monster! Run to that tent! Maybe they've got guns!"

Two screaming people charged up the ravine heading for the Gnairt's tent. At the same time two other shapes slipped from the back of the tent and fled through the trees.

Not the diversion any of us were expecting, but it worked. Anyway, this was our chance. Opal and I pelted down the slope and reached the tent just ahead of the two screamers. Leaping inside, we grabbed the stolen canvas sacks. I turned to see Melanie and Scott staring at us, wide-eyed, through the tent opening.

"What are you two doing here?" Opal said.

"We didn't believe you," Scott gasped. "We followed you and . . . What is that thing out there? It's coming this way!"

"What thing?" I asked innocently.

"Like a dinosaur," Melanie wailed. "With lots of teeth!"

"Oh, that," I said, looking around desperately, stalling for time. Several alien devices were scattered around the tent. I grabbed one randomly. Probably just a Gnairt can opener, but it *did* look pretty impressive. "That's just my laser holographic projection. I create it with this gizmo. I wanted to scare away the thieves so we could grab the rocks. But I guess you ran into the image first and instead scared them for us."

Opal looked at me, obviously impressed. So was I.

I shouldered one of the sacks and thrust the other at Scott. "Let's split before they come back."

The four of us scrambled up the ravine. I stayed in the lead, keeping an eye on the trees ahead of us and the just-visible flicking of Vraj's tail. Eventually it led us to a different path, one that ran around the lake toward camp.

We walked for a while without saying anything. Then Melanie's voice broke the silence. "Sorry we didn't believe you, Opal."

"That's OK," the pudgy little girl replied. She was swinging along with a more confident step, and I could almost feel her radiating happiness.

"That sure is a cool projection thing you have," Scott said. "It convinced us all right." He laughed sheepishly.

With my free hand, I patted the little can opener or whatever it was that I'd stuck in my belt. "My dad's a scientist. He thought I'd have fun with this thing at camp."

"Hey, Zack," Opal said. "Where are we going to hide these things so the bad guys don't steal them again?"

I frowned. "The camp buildings aren't safe, it seems. What we need is to dig a big hole and bury them until . . . until they're taken away. But we don't have the time or the shovels."

"Hey, I know," Scott said, "if you don't mind a suggestion."

I almost liked Scott now that he was deflated a little. "Out with it."

"We Sports Sprites had a water sports fest

and Hawaiian luau yesterday. We dug a big hole up by the fire circle for roasting yams. It's not filled in yet."

"Then that's where we're headed," I said, veering to the right.

It wasn't long before we reached the fire circle, dumped the sacks into the luau pit, and filled it in from the pile of loose dirt. Then we sat on the fire circle logs, tired and dirty, but not yet ready to go back to our cabins.

And now we had an added complication. These two new recruits, though they knew less of the truth than Opal, could still mess things up. I'd caught a glimpse of Vraj hiding behind a bush, and I knew she'd be fretting about a security leak.

I cleared my throat. "Scott and Melanie, I'm sorry you got scared and all, but could I ask a favor? Could you keep quiet about this?"

"Sure thing," Scott said. He probably didn't want people to know that Mr. Big-Man-about-Camp had been scared witless.

"I won't tell either," Melanie said, then

switched to a wheedling voice. "But could I ask a favor back?"

"What?" I asked cautiously.

"Well, we Arts Angels are supposed to come up with individual projects, poetry or painting or something. I should do something theatrical of course, since that's my art, but I can't think of a thing. If I . . . if we put together a show using that laser projector, it would be a real hit."

"Yeah," Opal said excitedly, then clapped a hand over her mouth, probably just realizing there *was* no laser projector.

Scott jumped in. "Right, and if we offer parts to the others in our cabins, they'll keep quiet about our being out tonight. We'll say we were practicing."

"Yeah, but . . . " Opal began.

I waved her down. "Let me think a minute." The idea was crazy, but it sounded like fun. And now that my mission was wrapped up, I could use some fun.

I stood up. "OK, we could do a play about

the Greek myth Andromeda. Opal knows that stuff so she can write it. Melanie could be the star, of course, since it's her project, but we'd all have parts. We'll use that projector for the sea monster, Draco."

Opal giggled, the others applauded, and I sat back, hoping Vraj had overheard. She'd said it would take a while for the Patrol to come pick up the eggs, so she'd have the time. She might even enjoy this, and anyway, she owed these kids something for their help.

Everything, at last, seemed to be winding up nicely.

When, I wonder, am I going to learn?

CHAPTER SIX

Vraj definitely did not like the idea.

The next night I met with her at our regular spot, the hill of the lone pine. "You expect me to take part in stupid, childish native games?" she spluttered as moonlight glinted dangerously off her teeth.

"Lighten up," I said, averting my eyes from those teeth. "Your job here's nearly done."

"One egg's still missing," Vraj snapped as she paced around the tree.

Annoyed, I sat down on a fallen log. "Then look for it. Or maybe somebody miscounted. Anyway, the eggs are safe from hatching now, tucked away from light in that pit. You've got to wait around for the ship so you might as well have some fun."

"This will not be fun."

I shrugged. "OK, then it's *duty*. Planned or not, you've involved a lot of native kids in completing this mission. Opal has been a help, and it was Scott and Melanie who scared the Gnairt from their tent. And remember all those kids who collected your eggs? They deserve some payback. If you take the part of a laser-projected Draco, some of the kids will have fun doing the play and others will have fun watching it."

"As a member of the Galactic Patrol Corps, it's beneath my dignity to . . . "

"Bah. You're a Cadet. And is dignity more important than honor? Aren't you honor bound to help those who have helped you?"

Her grumbling wasn't translated, but finally she snarled, "All right, what do I do?"

"We have permission to rehearse during rest periods starting tomorrow. If you sneak down to the fire circle and watch, you'll see what's expected of Draco. It's easy. All you have to do is stalk up to Andromeda, look fierce, and threaten to eat her."

She grumbled again.

"Come on, I can't believe your species doesn't have plays."

"Of course we do! We have highly developed art forms. But this is . . . "

"This is your chance to be a star. Most members of the Galactic Patrol Corps never get a chance like this. And here you've lucked out on your first assignment."

She scowled but didn't contradict me. So I'd been right all along. This *was* her first assignment. She probably wasn't much older than me.

She kept grumbling like a small green volcano, but finally accepted the role.

For a couple of days, the play consumed the energies of two cabins, Opal's and mine. Bessy and Jessy were thrilled to be acting with a real, experienced actress, the Hollywood-bound Melanie. Following Scott's lead, even Ramon and Carlos got into it. Rehearsals were a bit ragged because not everyone had learned their lines, but Melanie flounced around like a temperamental director, shaming them into it. Occasionally I saw a flicker in the bushes. Our surprise cast member.

The campfire area on a bluff overlooking Lake Takhamasak made a good stage. Log seating sloped up from the flat clearing next to the fire circle. The luau pit had been in part of that clearing so some of the dirt was soft. However, most of the stage area was hard packed and perfect for acting. Bushes screened the area behind our stage.

On the night of our performance, everyone in the cast was almost too nervous to eat. I'd met with Vraj the night before, giving her special instructions. She still scorned the whole idea, but I thought her reptilian glare seemed less fierce than usual. A hint of excitement trying to break through?

The cast and the other performers at the

night's campfire were excused early from the dining hall. We rushed back to our cabins to put on costumes and then headed down to the fire circle. I stuck my Gnairt gizmo in the pocket of the old bathrobe I was wearing as my king costume. I had to make sure that everyone would think Vraj was a laser projection.

Nervously we checked the props: the thrones for the king and queen, the cardboard rock to tie Andromeda to, the yardstick swords, and of course, the Gorgon's head. Jessy and Bessy had built it from papier-mâché with rubber snakes stuck into it so they wriggled and bobbed.

As the first campers trooped toward the fire circle, we hid behind the bushes. On the excuse of checking my equipment, I slipped into another clump of bushes where Vraj was hiding.

"Nervous?" I whispered.

"Of course not!" Her voice seemed higher than usual.

"All great actors get nervous, you know. This could start a grand career for you."

She snorted. "I am going to be . . . I *am* in the Galactic Patrol."

"Well, everyone needs a hobby. Besides, if you have talent, it'd be wrong to deprive the universe of it."

"You really think I could have talent?"

"Sure. You'll knock 'em dead. Eh . . . that's just an expression."

She grinned, showing more teeth than any Hollywood star. "Right."

I joined the other cast members crouching and waiting. Once all the campers and counselors were seated, the campfire was lit, and everyone sang the Camp Takhamasak song. Then three girls sang songs by their favorite rock group. They did *not* have a future in music. Next came a boy who juggled pinecones and tin cups. Judging by audience sounds, he only dropped things twice.

Then it was us. My stomach tightened. Opal looked like she was going to be sick.

"You'll do fine," I whispered. "If actors don't get stage fright, the show wouldn't have any zip." At the moment, it looked like Opal wanted to zip right out of there. I kept a grip on her arm and whistled for Ramon and Carlos to make their entrances.

Dressed as soldiers, they stepped from the bushes. Their armor was cheesy-looking aluminum foil stuff, but their stick and cardboard spears looked OK. Scott, crouching beside me, beat dramatically on a drum. Several kids in the audience jeered at the soldiers, but counselors hushed them.

I practically had to push Opal out onto the stage. She began her speech about constellations in a really tiny voice. Someone in the audience yelled, "louder!" That must have made her mad because she started belting out her lines. Scott banged his drum again. Opal scurried back and threw on her wig and dress. Then she and I strode out as King Cepheus and Queen Cassiopeia.

We sat on our thrones, and, to more drum banging, Melanie, in the role of Andromeda, skipped out wearing a floaty nightgown thing.

She was accompanied by Bessy and Jessy, playing servants. For no reason I can figure out, those two launched into a cheerleader routine, waving pine branches and flipping up their little skirts. Through this ridiculous routine, Opal and I gushed about how beautiful our daughter was. I could have gagged. Melanie must have helped write those lines.

Finally Opal rose and yelled, "Andromeda is even more beautiful than the sea nymphs, Neptune's daughters!"

That's when Scott, behind the bushes, bashed the garbage can to sound like thunder. The last thwack was so hard I heard the can topple and bounce noisily down the hill. Scott couldn't stop it because he was busy making his entrance. He was the god Neptune, in a green sheet with shredded bits of garbage bag trailing off him to look like seaweed.

It was a grand entrance, except that he stepped on his costume and fell on his face. Scott pulled himself to his knees. His face turned from dust-powdered pale to blush red as laughter from the audience rose in a wave. He jumped up, waving his pitchfork menacingly and shouted, "Whoever laughs at the great god shall feel his wrath after the show!"

The audience quieted. For a moment, Scott's face blanked as he fumbled for his real lines. I breathed again when he finally turned to us and thundered, "Whoever compares the beauty of a mere mortal to my daughters shall feel the wrath of the great god Neptune!"

That was our cue to scream and wail and fall on our knees, begging forgiveness. Bessy and Jessy flailed frantically, and not to be out-done, Melanie threw herself on the ground and flopped about like a dying fish.

Then came a bunch of talk where nobody quite got their lines right, but in the end Neptune agreed he would not send his sea monster, Draco, to destroy the town, if we tied Andromeda to a rock for Draco to eat instead. More screaming and wailing, then everyone ran into the bushes.

The audience cheered and clapped and started to leave until Scott ran out waving his pitchfork and yelling, "Sit down! There's more coming!" When some kids groaned, he added, "Shut up! We've got special effects!"

Once they settled down, Andromeda entered slowly followed by the soldiers prodding her with spears. Then came the two wailing servants and the king and queen. Opal and I were dressed in black garbage bags that were supposed to make us look like we were in mourning. I think they made us look like walking garbage bags.

Andromeda was tied to the cardboard rock. More screaming and wailing, and the two servants did a sad little dance. Very sad, if you ask me. Then we all trooped off except Melanie, who stayed tied to her rock, trying to look scared and beautiful.

Meanwhile, Scott, crouching behind the bushes, had torn off his Neptune costume and put on aluminum foil armor and a colander helmet to play the part of Perseus. Ramon and Carlos struggled into their Pegasus costume. (They'd agreed to play the flying horse only if they could be soldiers at the beginning.) Ramon had lost the coin flip and gotten stuck with the role of the horse's butt. Carlos walked upright, holding the cardboard horse head. Ramon trudged along, bent over with a yarn tail pinned to his rear, while he flapped the cardboard Pegasus wings. Scott walked between them, "riding" Pegasus and trying to look heroic.

Pretending to not see Melanie, they staggered on stage to hoots of laughter. Scott fumbled through his speech about how he, Perseus, was just coming back from killing the Gorgon, whose glance turned people to stone. "Sounds like our counselors," some kid yelled. Then Scott got good squeals when he wiggled the snake-covered head at the audience.

Now came the special effects. Opal had crawled out of the bushes and thrown a bunch of pine needles and sand on the fire to make sparks and to lower the light. Backstage I was making a big deal of waving my gizmo and pretending to press buttons. Then from behind the bushes, we all started moaning, "Oooo, Draco the Sea Monster! Here comes the terrible monster! Andromeda is doomed! Doomed!"

On cue, Vraj burst out of the bushes. I've got to admit, she looked plenty scary. And mad too. I hoped she was just acting. She looked mad enough to eat somebody for making her do this.

The effect, though, was great! People screamed and cried and cheered. Vraj must have liked that. She made the most of it by running up and down aisles, flailing her claws, and snapping her teeth. Then she bounded back onstage and stalked toward Andromeda. Melanie's screams were very realistic. For a second I even thought she might run off, bouncing her cardboard rock behind her.

Vraj was making frightful snarls when Scott snapped out of his shock and urged his stumbling Pegasus forward. Pretending to jump off, he pulled out his yardstick sword and waved it timidly at Draco.

Vraj ignored him and kept gloating over miserable Melanie. Scott lunged forward, wiggling the sword in Vraj's face.

Explosively, Vraj spun around, yanked the sword away from Scott, held it in her front claws, and broke it in two. Watching through the bushes, I was impressed. I'd just told Vraj to do what fit the part. She was a natural.

Perseus yelped and jumped back. It was probably not the reaction he'd expected from a "projection." I'd have to think of some way to explain that later. Draco followed, claws outstretched, jaws gaping. Turning with a convincing scream, Perseus ran into the audience. Then he seemed to remember that this was a play and unhooked the dangling Gorgon head from his belt. Slowly he walked towards Draco, who was back slathering over Andromeda.

The audience was yelling, laughing, and screaming with delight. But I was worried. I wasn't sure if Vraj understood about the Gorgon's head. We hadn't rehearsed that part since most of the cast thought it would just be a projection. Timidly, Perseus stepped forward and wiggled the head at Draco. Nothing happened, though I caught a questioning look in the alien's eye.

"It turns things to stone," I whispered loudly under the audience's screaming. "You turn to stone and die!"

With a sharp nod, Draco turned and stared directly into Medusa's ugly papier mâché face. Then she squealed like a fire siren and began leaping about like she was being attacked by bees. She flailed to the back of the stage and with one final shriek, fell like a stone into the bushes and rolled out of sight.

For a moment, we were all stunned. Then I remembered I was the king. Singing happy praises for Perseus, I strode from the bushes with the others trailing me. Perseus untied Andromeda, they hugged briefly, and we all danced around the fire circle.

That was supposed to be the end of the show.

We had circled the fire for the third time

when I felt the soft earth move under my feet. It buckled and heaved like an earthquake in mush.

Suddenly the ground quaked, toppling me and the others to the ground. The soil, where we lay, churned with orange arms that broke free and began spiraling into the air. All around us, there were dozens of orange starfish-things the size of saucers. They swarmed into the air and swirled about like moths around a light. Then the swarm changed direction, and they sailed off into the night. The cloud of orange stars glided over the lake and disappeared beyond the trees.

After awed silence, the camp exploded with cheers. What special effects! A Greek myth turned into stars—right before our eyes! Kids happily slapped me on the back. I just stood in stunned horror.

The Duthwi eggs. The heat of the campfire. They'd hatched! Duthwi were loose on Earth, they and their mysterious menace. I'd totally botched my mission!

Beyond the bushes, I glimpsed a yellow-green streak—Cadet Vraj bolting down the hill and along the lakeshore. Everyone kept congratulating me.

I'd never felt more miserable in my life.

CHAPTER SEVEN

All the next day, the camp was buzzing about the show. Kids said I ought to go to Hollywood if I could do special effects like that. That annoyed Melanie, who felt *she* ought to go to Hollywood after her wonderful acting. I told her that anyone who could work a computer could do special effects, but not everyone had acting talent like hers. It wasn't true, but it cheered her up.

Nothing could cheer me up, though. I'd really messed up big time.

I wanted to run out and help, but I didn't know how. My last glimpse of Vraj was her sprinting after the flying Duthwi, but I hadn't a clue where they were now. And I didn't know if the mysterious Duthwi menace came when they were newly hatched or if they had to grow up first. All I could do was wait for Vraj to contact me.

At Nature Nuts I just grunted when Opal gushed privately about our wonderful acting dinosaur and my great star effects though she couldn't figure out how I'd done it. I kept mysteriously quiet. When rest time came, I slipped alone into the woods.

There, everything was quiet and peaceful. Only a few birds chirped sleepily, and even the insects sounded soft and drowsy. The air smelled spicy with pine and warm earth. I walked and walked without paying attention to where.

Slowly I noticed that something felt different. The drowsy quiet had slipped into uneasiness. Birds cried sharply overhead. I stared around and realized the trees here looked like they'd been blasted by lightning or hit by a tornado. Splintered wood lay everywhere. Trees rose halfway up, then ended in jagged spears.

What could have caused this? The patch of destruction was maybe thirty yards wide, and beyond it, the regular forest took up again. I was picking my way through the mess when suddenly the explanation was in front of me.

A hole had burned right through a tree trunk—a hole the shape of a star.

That's what Sorn had meant about environmental danger. Duthwi ate trees. They destroyed them. And I'd loosed a bunch of them on the world! If they spread and laid more eggs, think of the damage they'd do! Oh, well done, Agent Zack.

I spotted a little brook running through the blasted patch, half choked with splintered wood and pine needles. Listlessly I followed it down the hill until it ran into living forest again. Then I sat on a mossy rock and stared gloomily into the silvery water.

Time passed. Gradually I realized the light

and shadow on the stream had shifted. Ripples made one of the sunlit rocks look like it was moving. I stared. It *was* moving! It looked like a lumpy potato, and one of those lumps was throbbing.

Slowly I reached out and grabbed the thing. It was warm in my hands. I watched as parts bulged in and out and little cracks snaked over the surface. The whole thing shuddered, and bits of the surface fell off. Orange stuff underneath wiggled like jelly.

Suddenly it shook like a wet dog, and chunks of shell flew everywhere. An orange blob burst upward and splattered onto my cheek. It stuck.

"Mama!"

"I'm not your mama!" Was this thing talking to me? I didn't hear any sound, but the translator in my ear was tingling.

"Mama, Mama, Mama!"

I reached up and tried to pull the thing away. Its gooeyness was beginning to harden—into the shape of a star.

"Mama, Mama, Mama, where are others?"

"Wha . . . what . . . " I stuttered. "What others? Oh. The other Duthwi?"

"Brothers and sisters. Miss them. Lonely."

"I don't know where they are, but if you get off my cheek, I'll get you something to eat."

Instantly the thing dropped into my hand, a little orange star about the size of my palm.

"Hungry!"

"Right." I picked up a piece of tree bark and put it in the middle of the little star. Its points closed around the chip, and in seconds the bark was dust.

"More!"

I fumbled for a larger chunk of bark and laid it amid the wiggling orange arms. They snapped closed, and soon that piece was gone too.

"Sleep now."

The star closed in a tight ball and stopped wiggling. Astonished, I stared at the little thing. It must think I'm its mother because it saw me before anything else. I decided I'd better keep little Starry happy until I could find Vraj.

I put the little orange ball in my jacket's roomy pocket and added some shredded bark.

Picking up a few more chunks for backup, I hurried back to camp. Rest period was just ending. I slipped into the cabin as the others left, pulled my pack from under the bunk, and transferred the sleeping Duthwi inside. Then I stuffed all the bark I had into the pack, shoved it back, and hurried off to afternoon Nature Nuts.

It was now easier to avoid being latched onto by Opal, because after the play she'd become almost popular. So I had all the mental time I wanted to worry.

Before dinner, I checked on Starry. It was sleeping again after eating all the bark. I went outside to scrounge up some more, put that in the pack, and went off to dinner. My plan was to sneak out that night, taking the little Duthwi to the lone pine tree in hopes that Vraj would show up.

Of course, those plans did not work out.

Before going to bed, while the others were trooping to or from the latrine, I pulled out my pack. It was empty except for a star-shaped hole on one side. Frantically I looked under the bed. No Duthwi. But there was a star-shaped hole in the cabin's wooden wall. One hundred percent failure.

In agony, I lay in my bunk until my cabin-mates were finally asleep. Then I managed to sneak out. I half wanted to find Vraj at the tree and half dreaded it. But she wasn't there. I sat and waited. Shivering in the chilly air, I gloomily watched the stars. The sky across the lake was lit by a faint display of northern lights. Cool maybe, but I wasn't in the mood to be thrilled by nature. Even Opal's chatty presence would have been welcome. But I was totally alone, and the more alone I felt, the more I began to worry about Vraj.

Sure, she was a conceited grouch, but she was also a lone alien given a tough job on what to her must be a completely strange and dangerous world. Besides, she was just a kid. Finally, though, even worry couldn't keep me awake. I slunk back to the cabin and into a restless sleep.

The next day, everyone at the camp seemed a little down. It was the last full day of camp that session, and even those kids who'd been homesick at first didn't want to leave now. An extra-big campfire was planned for that evening, but I wasn't in the mood for even thinking about fun.

In the afternoon, I trailed behind the others on our last nature hike. I didn't feel very chummy either. Suddenly something slammed into my head.

"Mama!"

"Starry!" I cried from the ground, where I was sprawled with a starfish thing plastered to my forehead. It seemed to have grown.

"Mama, found brothers and sisters. They trapped. Bad people trap them. Got to help!"

Its vocabulary had grown too. "OK, OK.

I'll help. But you've got to let loose. And don't fly off, you need to show me where to go."

"OK, I stay. But hungry!"

It peeled itself off and walked down my face like a big, fleshy orange spider. Swinging my patched knapsack off my back, I stuck in some bark and twigs and urged the little Duthwi to crawl in. I'd just reshouldered my pack when Opal and Walt, the kid who'd given the talk about nighttime animals, came walking back down the trail.

"We just noticed you were missing," Walt said. I was glad to see he'd gotten chummy with Opal.

"What's that big red mark on your forehead?" she asked.

"Oh. I ran into a branch. I have an awful headache. I think I'll go to the nurse." I avoided actually looking at Opal. I knew that if she guessed this was a cover story, she'd want to go along. But with Gnairt involved, things could get dangerous. Anyway, this was *my* mess to clean up.

At the nurse's I complained of a migraine headache. My mom gets those, so I knew how to fake one. I said light hurt my eyes, and I saw lots of glowing wiggly lines. The nurse had me lie down in a dark room and said no one was to bother me for several hours.

Once she left, I reached into my pack. Most of the bark and twigs were gone, but the warm little star was still there.

"Go help others now?"

Before I could say anything, it had scrambled up my arm and under my shirt, settling onto my shoulder. It didn't really hurt, having the Duthwi stuck there, but it tingled like when my mother rubs smelly ointment on my chest when I get a cold.

"Right," I said. "We're going to help now. But where are they trapped?"

"Other side. Big water."

At the window, I pushed aside the curtains and looked out. This was the back of the nurse's building, facing the woods. Unlatching the window, I pushed it open. Then I spied some crayons and paper on a table and scrawled a quick note, saying I felt better and had gone to join the other campers. That way no one would look for me for a while.

In the woods, I avoided paths, but when I reached the lake, I realized my clever planning had petered out.

Lake Takhamasak was not small. But somehow I had to get to the other side and rescue hungry little aliens from bigger nasty aliens who probably had terrible weapons. My only ally was a snotty alien dinosaur who I hadn't seen in days. The Gnairt might have even killed her by now.

No, this was not a fun summer, I said to myself as I started trudging along the shore.

CHAPTER EIGHT

Waves lapped gently against the sand as I marched along. I stepped over a groove left earlier by a canoe, then stopped. I could canoe across the lake!

I looked back along the shore. The camp's dock wasn't far. And I knew how to canoe. Sort of.

Keeping a wary eye out for counselors or campers, I trotted back. The canoes were pulled up on the sand and turned over. The first one I came to was wooden and looked heavy as a tank, but the next was light. I flipped it over and hauled it to the water.

"What doing?" The tingly voice filled my

mind. Starry must have been sleeping on my shoulder.

"I'm borrowing a boat so we can cross the lake."

"Hurry. You so slow!"

"I'm going as fast as I can. I can't fly, you know." I shoved the canoe half into the lake, then looked it over. "Can't canoe either. No paddle. I'll have to go look for one."

"No time. I paddle!"

"Oh sure." I'd just spied a broken paddle on the sand and decided to take it rather than risk anyone catching me in the boathouse.

My feet got soaked when I launched the boat, but soon it was gliding into the lake, screened from the camp by a rocky point of land. Sports Sprite Scott would have jeered to see me handling the canoe. I kept switching the stubby broken paddle back and forth to keep us in a slow, crazy zigzag.

"Too slow, Mama!"

Like an itchy whirlwind, Starry crawled out of my shirt and down my arm. It examined the paddle, took a huge bite out of the blade, and then crawled along the side of the canoe to the back.

"Hey, don't eat the paddle! How am I supposed to make this boat move?"

"I paddle."

And it did, sort of. Starry climbed down the boat's stern to the waterline, held on with two arms and began kicking with the others. Slowly we moved forward. It kicked faster and faster until we were shooting along like a paddle-wheel steamer. I remembered how earlier I'd been annoyed that I wasn't getting a chance to canoe at this camp. Be careful what you wish for!

My hair blowing back, I crouched low, held onto both sides, and watched the far shore come closer. Closer and closer.

We weren't slowing down! "Whoa! Stop paddling!" Starry did just in time to send the canoe scraping way up onto the beach.

Shakily, I climbed out. "Thanks. I'll walk now."

"I fly. Hurry!"

Starry spun in the sand then shot into the air like a small orange helicopter. In moments it had disappeared over the trees. Some guide.

Leaving the pebbly beach, I walked through

tall grass, then into the trees, trying to catch a glimpse of orange. All I saw were dark pines and shafts of late afternoon sun.

Abruptly the trees stopped. I found myself standing at the top of a cliff looking down into a landscape as bare as the moon's. It was a wide, gray valley dotted with piles of gravel, rusty machinery, and a few small buildings. Surely even Duthwi couldn't make a place this bare. It was an old gravel quarry, I realized.

Just then, a small pine branch crashed down beside me. I looked up. My friend was snacking through a tree.

"Hey! I thought you were in a hurry."

In a shower of sawdust, Starry landed on my head. "Paddling hard work. Need food. Hurry now. Follow me!"

It sailed into the air in front of me, maybe fifty feet above the bottom of the pit.

"No way!" I muttered, looking down the sheer cliff. But there was a way, and I knew it. The problem is that it's easier to accept the idea of being an alien as long as it's just an *idea*, as long as you're not doing weird alien things.

I sighed and lowered myself over the edge. I just had to let my alien instincts take over. "Don't think, don't think." I chanted Agent Sorn's words to myself as I climbed down. Somehow toes and fingers found tiny chinks in the rock, and in moments I was at the bottom. Lizardman strikes again.

An orange speck dropped from the blue sky, buzzed over me, shot off to where the gravel pit turned a corner, and then disappeared. Keeping to the cliff's shadow, I ran in the same direction.

At the rocky corner, I peered around into another section of the gravel pit. This wasn't quite as deserted. There were several sheds, a cinderblock building, and a few empty gravel trucks. There was also, quite clearly, a spaceship.

Not that I'd ever seen a spaceship before, but there are some things you just can't mistake. Also, several creatures were moving near it, creatures that looked like they *ought* to be near a spaceship. They also looked like creatures you didn't want to see up close if you didn't have to. I had to, of course.

On hands and knees, I crept for a ways behind a low rock spur that finally gave out near the remains of a rusty mobile home. Peering around the wreck, I could hear the creatures near the spaceship talking, but I couldn't catch what they were saying.

To get closer, I slithered snakelike through the dust until I was crouched behind a stack of metal barrels. It was still nothing but gargling until, with a sharp pain in my ear, the translator kicked in. The first voice was high and oily. I shivered. A Gnairt.

"Eighty is the number of Duthwi we have to offer. Not a full hatching, perhaps, but more than you're likely to get a crack at in any hunting park, legal or illegal. Give us the money, and we'll release them. In a few hours they'll be dispersed and will be as challenging a hunting game as you'll find anywhere in the universe!"

The next voice was watery and deep.

"The challenge is alluring, but what about the Galactic Patrol?" A horrid gurgle that must have been a laugh. "Not that we Flaaa have any problems with breaking the law, we just do not relish getting caught. It is an annoyance."

"Would we allow our best clients to be annoyed?" Another Gnairt voice. "Should the Patrol appear, which is highly unlikely, we have the means to keep them at bay."

A gurgle rolled into words. "How? Your ship does not appear heavily armed."

"No. But as always, we Gnairt are armed with cunning, and that has given us two weapons to use. First, we have captured a Galactic Patrol officer, apparently the one they sent here to reclaim the eggs. Should the Patrol arrive and forbid your hunting, we simply threaten to kill her unless you are allowed to complete your hunt and depart without pursuit."

So that's what happened to Vraj! Captured by these slime.

The Flaaa grumbled. "But perhaps they would be willing to sacrifice one Patrol officer. Eighty is a fortune in rare, succulent Duthwi."

"Which is why we have a fallback. Should the Patrol continue to trouble your hunting pleasure, we have native hostages as well."

"Indeed? Are they imprisoned here too?"

"No need. See the weaponry mounted over there? It is trained on the far side of this lake, on a summer encampment of native young. Nearly a hundred of them. And remember, this planet is approaching the time of its invitation to join the Galactic Union. Mass slaughter of their young by aliens would not be a good introduction."

Flaaa laughter sounded like someone throwing up. Or maybe that image came to mind because that's what I felt like doing. Leaning against a barrel, I forced myself to think calmly.

OK. Vraj, the operative I was supposed to help, was captured and in danger of being killed. Bad. The Duthwi hatchlings I was supposed to protect were going to be killed for sport. Very bad. The place where my friends and fellow campers were staying might soon be blown off the planet. Very, very bad.

When I'd first realized that this was going to be a bad summer, I didn't have a clue just how bad bad could be.

CHAPTER NINE

The sky above the quarry glowed with sunset. Not that I could admire it at a time like this, but it told me I'd be losing light soon. Whatever I was going to do, I'd better do it now.

I crawled along the wall of barrels for a better look at the speakers. Immediately I wished I hadn't. Through a gap, I saw two Gnairt and one creature that must have been the Flaaa. Gnairt I'd seen before—none too handsome, but they look basically like fat, bald humans. Flaaa, however, were why the word "ugly" was invented.

This guy was a large puke-colored slug. Lumpy arms bulged out of his body wherever he needed them and then sank back in while another arm popped out somewhere else. Mostly those come-and-go arms seemed to be juggling a weapon-looking thing or scratching patches of undulating skin.

If I'd had time, I would have been sick right there.

I had to find where they were holding Vraj and somehow free her. Slowly I crawled backwards. I'd almost reached the shelter of a rusty piece of machinery when something grabbed my shoulder.

"Mama!"

Good thing I was too petrified to scream.

"I take you to others."

"Wait," I whispered. "I need to find someone else first. They've captured someone who could help us. She looks like a dinosaur. No, you wouldn't know that. She's yellow-green, she walks on two hind legs, and she has little front legs with claws, a long thick tail, and a big head with lots of teeth. Have you seen her?"

"No."

"Oh." Where was I going to look for Vraj in this huge place?

"Not seen, but know where she is."

"Huh?"

"Hear very angry yellow-green thoughts. Show where."

Starry zipped off low to the ground. I tried to keep up, but to my growing horror, we seemed to be heading toward the spaceship. I couldn't break Vraj out of *that*. They probably had high-tech security systems and weird alien locks.

I crouched beside a wooden shed near the ship, trying to build up courage. Starry dropped on my head. "Hurry ! Yellow-green person inside."

"Right. But I'm not sure I can break into a spaceship."

"What spaceship? Yellow-green person inside wood place."

"In this shed?" Hesitantly I knocked on the plank I was leaning against. From inside came scrabbling, thumping, and muffled growling.

Cautiously I circled the building till I found a door, a normal wooden door with a very non-normal lock. The whole thing seemed to be sealed with metal tape. I tugged and kicked at it but nothing happened, except the growling inside became more frantic.

"Mama want yellow-green person out of wood place?"

I nodded.

"OK."

The dish-sized orange star splatted itself against a wall and, in a spray of fine sawdust, chewed right through. It chewed another hole on the way back out and another going in again. In seconds, it had made a hole that was big enough for me.

"Nyuk! Wood, very stale."

"Sorry. But thanks." Kicking in a few jagged bits, I crawled through. The shed had only one small, dusty window, and the day's fading light was even weaker inside. But from the growling and thrashing, it was clear where Vraj was.

"Calm down. It's me, Zack." I walked toward the heaving lump. My eyes had adjusted to the gloom enough to see that Vraj had been thoroughly tied and gagged. Metal tape bound her arms, legs, and jaws, but her tail still thwacked about.

"Hey, watch where you swing that thing! There ought to be a way to get you loose." The Duthwi couldn't eat through the tape since it wasn't wood, but there were lots of tools hanging on the shed walls. In the shadows, I made out saws, hammers, and a metal snipper. Grabbing that, I knelt beside Vraj. She thrashed even harder.

"Hold still!"

The tape around the ankles was the loosest. Gripping a leg with one hand, I wriggled the blade of the snipper under the stretched tape, trying not to shudder at the feel of hard, slick skin. It wasn't like a snake's, though. It was warm, almost hot.

After several snips, the tape frayed, then snapped. Next I did the wrists, then, with more difficulty, the jaw. That might have been a mistake. She started complaining right away.

"About time someone got here! I've been tied up for two days! I'm starved!"

A worrisome statement from someone with teeth like that, but I tried to ignore it.

"Food comes later. Right now, we've got to rescue the Duthwi before the Gnairt turn them over to some really gross hunters."

"Looks like they're free already," Vraj said, watching Starry bouncing around the shed, sampling wooden tool handles.

"That's the missing Duthwi egg. It hatched out and got the crazy idea I'm its mama. But it led me here and knows where the others are being held."

"Duthwi are supposed to be smart as well as tasty," Vraj commented. I hoped Starry hadn't picked up on that last part.

The hole in the wall was small for Vraj, but she forced her way through, further splintering the edges. Soon we were both trotting behind the flying starfish. The sunset brilliance had faded, but the sky arching over us was streaked with purple and deep crimson.

The Gnairt near the metal barrels had switched on a greenish light. We passed close enough to hear rumbling voices. "Ah, so it's Flaaa they're dealing with," Vraj hissed when she heard the oily tones. "They're rich enough to pay the Gnairt's price."

Our little guide, flying low to the ground, kept zooming ahead and zooming back when we couldn't keep up. Its orange skin glowed slightly, enough at least for me to keep it in sight. As we approached several low buildings, Starry dropped onto my shoulder again.

"Mama, others in here. Hurry, get them out!"

The cinderblock building ahead of us was an abandoned ruin with a tree growing through a gaping hole in the roof. We peered through a doorway. Darkness was lit by a faint orange glow. In a far corner, a shapeless something glowed like a lumpy pumpkin. We crept closer. It looked like a large trash bag stuffed with glowing Duthwi. They were boiling and bulging around in there but couldn't get out.

Our free Duthwi zipped over our heads and landed on the bag, thumping it uselessly with its legs. Vraj and I crouched beside the bag. The surface felt smooth and cold like plastic, but Vraj's claws couldn't scratch it. I tried the metal snippers on a corner of the bag. Nothing.

"Don't you have some fancy alien weapons that could cut through this stuff?" I asked.

She snorted. "Of course, I *had* weapons, but the Gnairt took them when they threw me in the shed. We'll have to carry the bag."

That wasn't easy. Duthwi in large numbers are heavy. And bouncing around like that, they kept shifting the weight, nearly knocking us over as we lifted the sack onto our shoulders.

"Tell your friends to stop moving around!" I snapped at Starry.

But all Starry said was "Eeeeeee!"

That squeal lanced through me. I stumbled,

and the whole bag fell on me. Muffled through its squirming contents, I heard a Gnairt voice. "Got away, did you? Not this time!"

A sizzle of weapons' fire fried the air above me. Desperately I fought my way out from under the bag. Vraj had ducked behind a cinderblock wall. The Gnairt fired at her again. A chunk of wall exploded in dust, but Vraj leapt free. She landed on the tree and scrambled toward the gap in the roof. The Gnairt aimed again.

Yanking the metal snipper from my pocket, I threw it. I'd aimed at the bald head but only hit a shoulder. Still, the energy shot went wild, missing Vraj and shearing off a tree branch. Now, however, Vraj had time to escape and the Gnairt was looking at *me*.

I turned to run for the doorway, but the fat shape of another Gnairt blocked it. Nowhere to go but up. Leaping over the bag of squirming Duthwi, I bounded toward the tree. An energy blast exploded in front of me, setting one end of the fallen branch on fire.

Grabbing the other end, I swept up the burning branch, meaning to throw it at the nearest Gnairt. One blazing twig nicked the bag.

"Eeeeeeeeeeee!" The sound was piercing. That patch of bag melted, and all the Duthwi burst free. The little building filled with panicky, flying starfish. Some shot out the hole in the roof. Some poured out the door, knocking that Gnairt to the ground. As he scrambled to his feet, the other Gnairt joined him, and they both ran out. I followed.

The sky was dark now except for a swirling mass of orange stars. *Free to destroy Earth's trees again*, I thought grimly, but at least they wouldn't be sport for gross slugs.

Wrong. From back in the green-lit area, a thin red beam of light shot into the air. A soaring Duthwi plummeted down. One Flaaa was getting in his hunt anyway.

I didn't know what to do. Hide from the Gnairt? Go after the Flaaa? Look for Vraj? What I did was scream.

Two clawed hands grabbed me and yanked me to the roof of the cinderblock building. I'd found Vraj.

"Can't we stop them?" I gasped.

"We won't have to," Vraj yelled over the noise of firing weapons and screeching Duthwi. "They will."

I followed her gaze into the sky. Clustered blue lights were dropping out of the darkness.

"Just before the Gnairt caught me," Vraj said, "I got off a message to the Patrol. An Emergency Assistance Required message. Didn't want to. Kind of an admission of failure, but . . . " She made a gesture I guessed was a shrug. "Anyway, they've arrived, and the Gnairt and their client can't talk their way out of this! A clear violation of Galactic law. While they held me captive, they might have bargained, but now they've nothing to bargain with."

We'd just jumped to the ground when I remembered. "Oh yes they do have something to bargain with! Camp Takhamasak! I overheard them. They'll blow up the camp if they aren't let off!"

I was already running, though, without a clue what I could do. Vraj ran after me. Ahead, one Gnairt was running toward their ship, probably to send off their threat, while the other ran toward the cannonlike weapon mounted nearby. The only person *not* running was the Flaaa, who was gleefully shooting screaming Duthwi from the sky.

I pounded over the gravelly ground. Overhead, the remaining Duthwi banded together and shot off toward the lake. Ahead, one Gnairt had vanished into his ship while the other was fiddling with the weapon. He hadn't noticed me.

Crouching, I fumbled over the ground, grabbed a couple of rocks, and crept closer. In the dark, I heard scuffling behind me. Vraj must have been doing the same.

The nearly full moon had just cleared the eastern rim of the gravel pit. By its white light, we saw the Gnairt slam on a pair of earphones and drop into the gun's swivel seat. Unfortunately, he swiveled my way.

For a moment we just stared at each other. Then, with an evil grin on his bloated face, he drew a smaller gun and aimed at me.

I threw one rock and dove aside. An energy bolt sizzled through the air, grazing my hand with incredible pain. Gasping, I stuck that hand into my pocket and threw my last rock with the other hand. Then I sank, groaning, to the cold bare ground. There was nowhere to run and nothing to fight with. All I could do was play dead.

With the pain I was in, it didn't seem much like play. I just lay there in the moonlight, but the Gnairt seemed to have lost interest in me. My throbbing hand, cocooned in my pocket, felt something sharp and hot. The alien can opener. Great. But it hadn't been hot before. I glanced down. My whole pocket glowed.

Wincing, I pulled the thing out. One knob glowed pink. Had the blast from the Gnairt's gun triggered the change? What was this thing, really? Could it be a weapon?

I looked around. Hopefully Vraj was safe somewhere, but she wasn't near enough to give advice. The Gnairt had gone back to his cannon.

Overhead hovered the clustered blue lights of a Galactic Patrol ship. It had probably already received the Gnairt's demands: either let them and the rich slug go free, or they'd blow up a camp of native young—my friends, my people, even if they weren't my species.

Gingerly, I clutched the thing I'd pulled from my pocket. If this was really some sort of weapon, now was the time to use it. Shifting as little as possible, I slipped the gizmo to my good hand and aimed it toward the cannon. The pink knob was glowing brighter now. Ready to fire—or open a can.

Pulling myself up to a crouch, I pressed the knob. Nothing happened. Then I spun the thing around and pressed a silver knob. Still nothing. No, wait. The pink was getting brighter and shifting to purple. This gadget had to be a weapon. It had to work!

As I jabbed the knob again and again, the purple glow deepened and spread up my hand, my arm. Was this thing going to self-destruct? No! I had to destroy that cannon. I couldn't let them blast the camp. I couldn't let my and Vraj's mission fail so completely!

I seemed to be entirely purple now, glowing like a neon sign. The Gnairt at the gun turned and stared. Frightened and furious, I screamed like a karate guy. Purple energy shot out of my hand and through the air like a laser. It slammed into the mounted cannon.

The explosion was deafening. Its force blew me to the ground. I lay there, watching the most incredible fireworks. Then they and everything else faded to black.

CHAPTER TEN

Major motion sickness. Worse than a roller coaster. Worse than a fast car on curvy roads.

My head hurt, my stomach sloshed, and I was bouncing up and down. Slowly I opened my eyes. Everything was bouncing. Shadow, moonlight, trees. My arms were stretched over my head and hurting, like someone was gripping them. Someone with claws.

I snapped another notch awake. That "someone" was carrying me like a sack on her back. "Vraj!"

"About time you woke up. Support your weight! Grip my sides with your knees and grab my shoulders."

I tried. It was harder than horseback riding.

"Where are we going?"

"To your camp, out of harm's way."

"But the camp's going to be blown up!"

"Not now. You blew up their weapon, remember? Quite a show."

"Oh. Yeah." Things were falling into place. "So what's the danger now?"

"The Gnairt and Patrol ships are firing at each other, and we're in the middle. Now shut up. I need my breath for running with a heavy weight."

I'd rather have walked—if my wobbly legs could have held me. Anyway, the sizzling explosions behind us made speed seem like a good idea.

"Off!" Vraj ordered when we'd finally reached the main camp building. Gratefully I slipped off, but I almost collapsed and had to grab a log pillar for support. Slowly my legs began doing their job again. I turned to thank Vraj, but she was gone.

So was everybody else. Then I remembered

it was after dinner now, and they must be at the session's last campfire. I stumbled toward the fire circle.

At the crest of the hill, I gasped. The sky over the lake was lit up like the Fourth of July. Crisscrossing beams of light, red and blue, were highlighted with brilliant white bursts. The kids below me squealed and pointed excitedly.

Then came a massive explosion. Sky and earth shook with noise, and light blossomed over the lake like a fierce red flower. Chunks of flame and a curtain of sparks dropped to the water below. The remaining cluster of blue lights skimmed over the distant trees and disappeared.

Everyone cheered and clapped. "Best fireworks ever!" somebody yelled. "What a way to end camp!"

As I stumbled through the crowd, someone tugged my jacket. "Wasn't that show just wonderful?" Melanie cooed. "I hope you didn't miss it, sulking at the nurse's with a stupid headache."

Beside her, Scott grinned. "Nah, Zack knew all about it, I bet. His special effects stars started the show. That headache was just an excuse so he could help set it up. Great job, Zack!" He slapped me on the back, nearly toppling me over.

As those two swept off, there was Opal looking up at me, eyes wide and worried in her plump face. "What was that bit with the stars?"

"What bit?"

Her eyes widened further. "You really missed it? Just as the fireworks began, a swarm of those orange stars swept in from over the lake. They dove right into the campfire and completely burned up. The fire flared up in a big shower of sparks. Then there was a huge explosion across the lake, and the fireworks in the sky got bigger."

She grabbed my arm. "I've figured it out, though. Those stars weren't special effects. They were real—just like the dinosaur. They hatched out of those eggs, and then flew off somewhere and evolved into baby dinosaurs.

I bet what flew back and got burned up were really just empty shells. The babies are still out there, I bet. They're all right, aren't they?

Her eyes pleaded with me, wanting to believe this crazy explanation. I wanted to believe it too. But I didn't.

"Sure, you've figured it out," I said forcing a smile. "You'll make a great scientist."

Relief seemed to shower over her. "Will I get to see our dinosaur again?"

I shook my head. Some part of my brain still seemed able to churn out stories. "No, she's going back into hiding. But she sends her thanks. And you'll keep all this secret, right?"

"Totally! But when I'm a grown-up scientist, maybe I'll get to work with them."

"Maybe," I muttered as Opal skipped off to join her friends. And maybe when the Galactic Union decides Earth is ready to join them, everyone will accept aliens the way this kid accepted an "evolved dinosaur." I guess helping that happen is part of my job.

But the other part! My heart ached as I looked down at the smoldering campfire. The Duthwi must have felt that burning themselves up like moths was better than falling to greedy hunters. But it shouldn't have ended like that.

No one would call me Mama ever again.

I returned to the cabin in an exhausted daze, and nothing, not even my aching hand or my jabbering cabinmates, kept me awake.

The next morning we were to get on our buses right after breakfast. But as I halfheartedly speared my last canned peach, Muskrat, our counselor, came up to me.

"Don't get on the bus, Zack. We just got a call from your mother that your aunt is picking you up later."

That snapped me awake. My aunt? She wouldn't . . . Oh, my *Aunt Sorn*. She could probably imitate my mom if she needed to.

Then came the hauling of luggage and the tearful farewells. I'd actually miss some of those kids. Even Scott and Melanie had kind of grown on me. Opal gave me the secret dinosaur-claw sign before clambering onto the bus with her new friends. She wasn't the same Bashful the Dwarf who'd come here just a few days ago.

Finally, the last bus rumbled off in a smelly, dusty cloud. The camp was suddenly empty and quiet. While the remaining counselors bustled about, I sat at a dining-hall table, feeling alone and tired. My hand ached only a little. Not enough to keep me from resting my head on the table and almost drifting to sleep.

Someone sat down across from me. I jerked myself upright.

A handsome, white-haired lady smiled at me, my so-called Aunt Sorn. "Feeling all right? Ready to go?"

I nodded. "Just tired."

"I should think so after what our Cadet told me. That was a good job you did last night."

"Yeah, but it would have been better if the Duthwi hadn't all been shot or burned up."

"Come on." She stood up and walked

purposefully away from the dining hall. I sighed and followed.

Instead of the parking lot, we headed toward the campfire area. In the bright morning light, it felt cold and deserted. No—down by the fire circle, something was moving, digging like a dog, sending up plumes of ash. Vraj.

I hurried to her between rows of log seats. Scrabbling among ashes and charred wood, she was pulling out what looked like lumpy potatoes. Duthwi eggs.

I stared, confused. "But how?"

Sorn came up behind me. "Duthwi are attracted to heat and light. That must be how the Gnairt lured them into their trap."

I suddenly remembered what I'd taken to be northern lights across the lake. What a dummy! The lake was west, not north. I frowned. "But Duthwi are smart. Light is one thing, but why would they fly right into a fire?"

"Defense," Sorn answered. "When Duthwi are frightened, as they surely were by the Flaaa hunter last night, they try to escape. The most secure thing they can think of is being eggs again, and a really hot fire can turn a young Duthwi back into an egg. They saw this campfire and headed for it."

"Oh." I looked down at Vraj. "Why didn't you tell me Duthwi could do that?"

She snorted. "Hey, I'm new at this. I didn't know till she told me this morning. Now help me dig these things out."

The three of us raked through the ashes, pulling out sooty eggs and putting them in a shimmering metallic sack. I hoped that Starry was one of them and not one that the disgusting Flaaa had shot down.

As I put one more egg into the sack, the word "Mama" echoed with a familiar tingle in my mind. Smiling with relief, I held the egg in both hands.

"It's OK," I whispered to it. "You're going to a nicer place. Mama says so." I didn't know what the Duthwi home world was like, but I hoped it was wall-to-wall with fast-growing trees.

Sorn stood up, brushing herself off. "That's the lot. Now, Cadet, let's get them to your ship, and you can complete your mission by taking them home."

I offered to help, but Vraj stubbornly threw the sack over her shoulder like she'd done with me.

"You're strong," I said, "for an overgrown lizard."

She swatted me with her tail. A good-natured slap, I think.

Vraj's little ship was hidden among rocks and fallen branches on the hillside with the lone pine. From there, we could just see the roofs of the camp and glints of Lake Takhamasak beyond. Not a bad summer camp, even if it didn't have horses.

When we'd stowed the eggs, Vraj bowed formally and saluted her superior officer.

Sorn saluted in return. "Mission well done, Cadet Itl Vraj Boynyo Tg. You'll go far in the Galactic Patrol Corps."

Vraj nodded crisply, then turned to me. Her

usual yellow-green suddenly flickered to emerald. Was that a blush? "I couldn't have done it without help from this agent." Her beady yellow eyes looked into mine. "You'll go far too, Agent Zackary Gaither. Maybe we'll work together again."

Quickly she reached into her ship, pulled out something, and thrust it at me. "Here. You're quite hopeless at making your own." It was the beautiful little basket she'd made at Nature Nuts.

With that, she scuttled into her ship and slammed the hatch. The silver sphere rose silently into the air, the last dust and pine needles sifting from it. Then, in a barely visible streak, it shot into the blue morning sky.

After moments watching it, Sorn said, "Well, Zack, guess it's time you went home too."

I nodded, fumbling secretly in my pocket for a tissue. I found something else.

"Oh. Maybe I should give this to you." I pulled out the silvery Gnairt gizmo. "What is it anyway? I took it from their tent thinking

it was just something like a can opener. But I guess it's really some kind of weapon."

Sorn took it, looked it over, then tossed it back to me. "It's a can opener."

"But it . . . "

"It didn't do anything. *You* did. It has a little power cell meant for opening cans. You took that power, expanded it, channeled it, and used it as a weapon."

I felt cold and a little sick. "Like what happened before. You know, it's really scary being able to do that sort of thing but not knowing how. You keep saying I'm not ready for training yet, but could I maybe get a few pointers?"

She chuckled. "Maybe you should. The way things have been going on this planet, we may need a *trained* agent here earlier than we thought. We'll talk about it on the drive back. Though my hope is that for the next few years you'll get to live a perfectly normal human kid's life."

I followed her to the parking lot, not certain anymore that I totally shared that hope. Sure, discovering I was an alien agent with a weird alien mission had totally messed up my life.

But I had to admit it had been a pretty interesting summer.

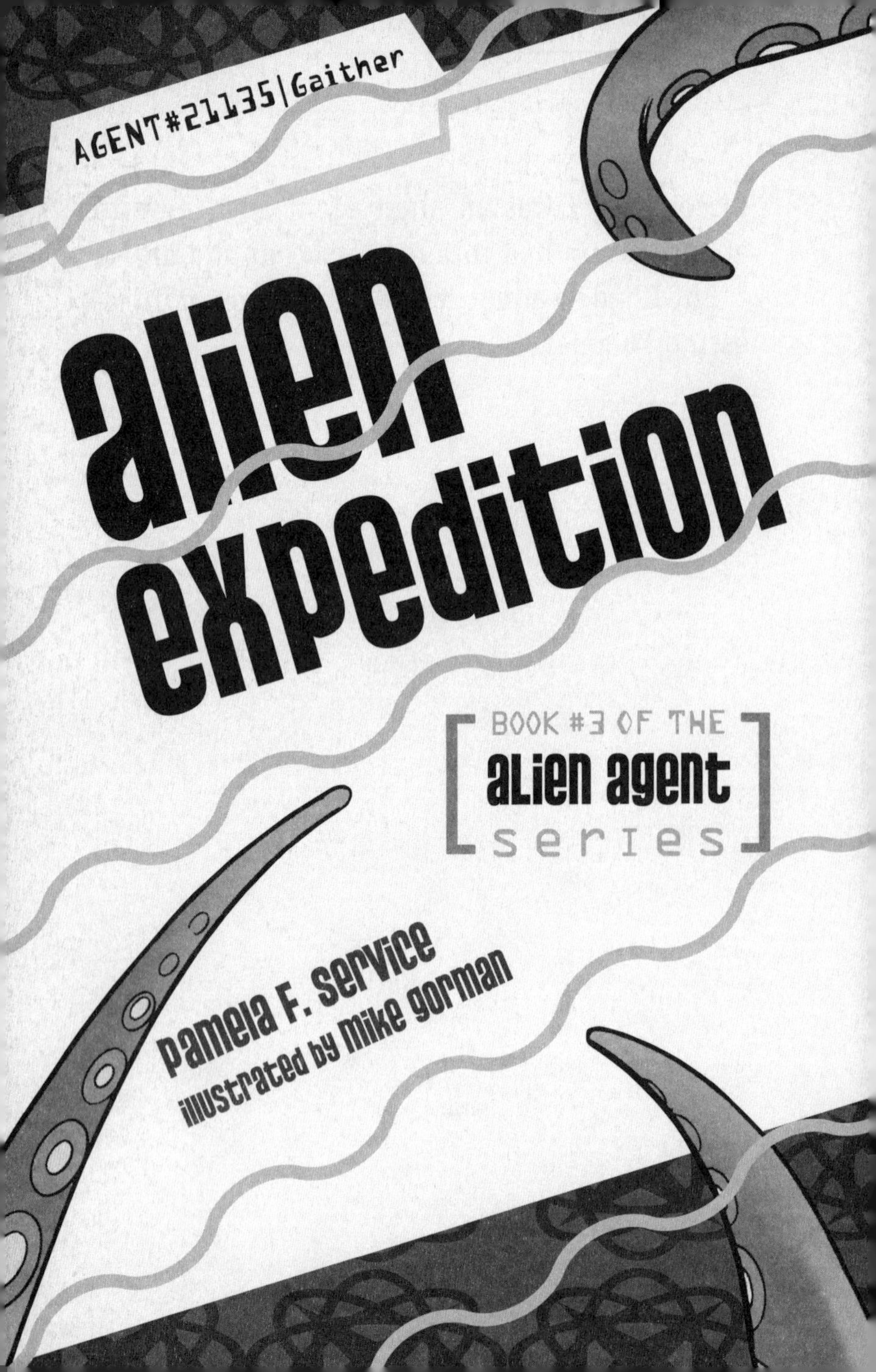

AGENT #21135 | Gaither
alien expedition
BOOK #3 OF THE
alien agent
series
Pamela F. Service
illustrated by Mike Gorman

TOP SECRET
from
ALIEN EXPEDITION

DOWNLOADING....

The summer was starting to look like a real bust. Until Alien Agent Sorn showed up, that is. After a slightly awkward handshake, we walked to the burger place near school. She said it was her treat, so I splurged on a root beer float and large fries.

"I really wish we didn't have to keep calling on you before you're older and fully trained," said Agent Sorn. "But something critical has come up on this planet. This new assignment should be easy, though. You probably won't have to do a thing besides enjoy a foreign vacation and be on hand just in case our other agent needs a bit of help."

"Sounds good," I said, dumping ketchup on my fries. "So where's this vacation?"

"Mongolia."

My hand jerked so much I sloshed ketchup on the white Formica tabletop. She might as well have said Mars or Alpha Centauri or something. "You mean, like over by China?" I said, as I hastily wiped up the ketchup with a wad of paper napkins.

"It is rather remote from your point of view, I suppose. We've arranged for your parents to be invited to join an American expedition to the Gobi Desert this summer. And of course you'll go along. It's a real scientific expedition doing an archaeological survey.

But it seems there's going to be another expedition there as well, unknown to anyone on this planet. It's from the Tirgizian Academy of Sciences. We tried to persuade them to hold off with their trip until the Galactic Union was ready to officially make contact with Earth. Unfortunately, they are not a patient people. And they have friends in high places, so their expedition is going ahead. They have sworn to keep their presence absolutely secret from the natives, but we thought it best to place an agent there to monitor things. And, as a backup to her, we need another agent who can work with humans in case anything goes wrong. That would be you."

"And your other agent can't work with humans?"

Agent Sorn smiled. "Well, she had a little trouble last year, I believe."

"Vraj? Yeah, I'd say looking like a vicious dinosaur does make it kind of tough getting along with people. How come you chose her?"

"She's Tirgizian herself. And she can handle whatever contact is needed between them and the Earth-based agent—you. At least I'm finally giving you an assignment where practically nothing can go wrong."

You'd think that I'd have learned by now not to buy that kind of line.

about the author

Pamela F. Service is the author of all the books in the Alien Agent series. She has written more than 20 books in the science fiction, fantasy, and nonfiction genres. After working as a history museum curator for many years in Indiana, she became the director of a museum in Eureka, California, where she lives with her husband and cats. She is also active in community theater, politics, and beach combing.